HEART
OF
FIRE

CONNOR WHITELEY

ACKNOWLEDGMENTS

Thank you to all my readers without you I couldn't do what I love.

CHAPTER 1

With the sun beaming down, Alessandria touched the back of her long neck. To feel the hot skin starting to turn red.

She rolled her eyes. She should have listened to her maid who wanted to force her to wear a cloak to cover up her skin on this hot day.

Now she was going to burn. Alessandria hated the servants being right, but that's why she loved them and wouldn't allow her mother to fire any of them.

To deal with the burning skin, she just flicked some of her long blonde hair over her neck.

Returning her attention to her task and purpose, she looked out over the market. To admire the rows upon rows of little wooden stalls with their owners and different goods. From the heavenly scents coming from the baker's stall to the hissing and banging of the blacksmith to the chatting of women and husbands at the jewellery stall. There was something here for everyone.

Alessandria continued to lean against the red brick wall to her right. The warmth of the bricks making it pleasant to lean against.

Stretching out her fingers, Alessandria felt the rough bricks that were starting to warm up as the afternoon started.

Looking at each of the stalls, Alessandria studied each and every person at the market. From the fit and healthy nobility of her fellow noble houses to the white tunic wearing lower class to the homeless people that used whatever money they could to buy food so they may live for one more day.

Alessandria felt anger flash across her face. She hated the way the other four noble houses treated their so-called 'lower class' so what if they didn't have Noble Blood, they were still great people given the chance. That reminded Alessandria she needed to walk through part of Ordericous that her family was responsible for. Best to remind the locals that she was there for them.

A wooden tapping sound came from behind Alessandria. Turning around, she was filled with great delight as she laid her eyes on a tall slim woman with long brown hair and fine features. Wearing a long sweeping black cloak of the Procurators with the symbol of her house over her breast.

The tapping sound continued as the woman tapped a strange brown wooden staff on the brick wall.

"So, you made it this morning, Hellen," Alessandria said, smiling at her partner.

"Ya sound surprised. I always come when ya call me,"

Alessandria's eyebrows rose.

"Hellen, I heard reports that you were

having… relations with a man last night. I doubted you would be here,"

The tapping stopped.

"Alexis, the reports are wrong. I would never have relations with a man. The Procurator Code prevents it. I am married to justice,"

"Ha," Alessandria laughed. "Thankfully, that rule only applies if you serve as part of the Queen's Procurators. As Dominus Procurator for the House of Fireheart, my officers do not have such restrictions,"

"Well, I'll have to transfer at some point,"

Alessandria returned to watching and inspecting the market. More people were coming and going with each second. Everyone was trying to buy their lunch or get whatever they needed before the later lunch crowds got all the good items.

"Why are we here?"

Alessandria ignored her friend. She was focusing on finding her target.

"Ya know there was a very pleasant man hanging about my chambers earlier. He still might be there if you're interested,"

Alessandria rolled her eyes. She loved her friend, but her sex drive was extreme. Alessandria wondered why the Queen did such a rule preventing her servants from having sex. If anything it only breeds higher sex drives!

"Hellen, we're here because there's a criminal who's been robbing homes on Fireheart land. I traced him to the market,"

"Where he sells his goods?"

"Yes, but not the goods you're thinking of,"

Hellen gave a cheeky grin.

"Why do ya need me? Ya only need me normally when the Queen is in danger,"

"I bought you here because this isn't Fireheart land. I don't have jurisdiction here,"

Alessandria narrowed her eyes on a crowd of workers.

"But this is Earther land, didn't your mother arrange for your brother to get married to their eldest son?"

"Correct but…" Alessandria started as the words dried in her mouth as she saw a slim man with dark skin wearing a dirty tunic. His face was narrow, but Alessandria focused on the massive blood red scratch on his left cheek.

"That man is with the scratch on his cheek is our man. Go to the other side of the market. I'll approach him. Be careful,"

Hellen nodded and walked away. Throwing up her grey hood as she went.

Starting to walk through the crowd, Alessandria carefully passed men and women all around her as these people chatted at the stalls.

The air was thick with sweat from the morning's work and the sound of coins and chatting filled her ears.

Alessandria continued to advance until her

target stopped on the edge of the market. He started talking to a baker.

She kept walking.

Two homeless women dressed in red rags with dirt covering their entire body sat in front of a stall next to the target.

Alessandria shook her head, not at the homeless people but at what they represented. She loved all the people on her family's land. Alessandria and her mother personally knew each of them by name and the thought that another noble family would allow their people to become homeless was disgusting.

The Dominicus Procurator thought about it long and hard. She could go up to the homeless women and give them a few coins. But the target might see her and run. It had taken Alessandria three days to find him.

She went for it.

Alessandria quickly glided through the crowd and went to the women. She passed them a few coins.

The man saw her.

He ran.

He charged through the market.

"Stop in the name of the House of Fireheart. Stop!"

Alessandria ran after him.

Pushing her way through the crowd.

The man ran as fast as he could.

He bashed people to the ground.

He grabbed bread and jewels and threw them at Alessandria.

She dodged them.

He got to the end of the market.

Alessandria jumped over a stall.

The man screamed.

Alessandria gained on him.

He whipped out a pistol.

Alessandria tried to tackle him.

She missed.

The cobblestoned ground scarping her skin.

He was about to escape when Hellen whacked him with her stick.

Bones cracked and the man screamed in agony.

Alessandria wandered over to the man and grabbed his arms. Tying them behind his back. Before giving him to Hellen.

"It's good ya called me Alexis,"

Alessandria gave Hellen a fatigued wave.

"What ya want me to do with him?"

"Take him to the Queen's booking Chamber. Have him,"

Hellen cocked her head.

"This is a Fireheart case,"

"Go, Hellen. I'll see you later. You have this one. Get your Dominus Procurator off your back,"

"Thank ya!"

With that Hellen pushed the man off towards the immense castle in the distance with its massive spires reaching into the sky.

Turning around to face the market and the rows of tall white huts around it, Alessandria stretched her back.

"That was exciting!" a familiar posh voice said.

Alessandria's eyes narrowed to see a tall well-muscled man approaching her. Wearing a sterile white pressed suit with golden threads.

In addition, to the slim, highly attractive woman on his arm wearing her typical white flowery dress.

"If it isn't my Praetorian Brother Justin and his forever lovingly finance Annalise," Alessandria exclaimed as she straightened her back and attempted to make herself look presentable.

Justin and Annalise strolled up to Alessandria regally and gave her a quick hug, being careful not to get dust on themselves.

Alessandria looked around.

"Is mother with you? Or did you lost Mother again instead of protecting her, Praetorian,"

"No, my dearest sister. Mother is back at the castle. She gave me the afternoon off protecting her,"

"And we're going wedding dress shopping!" Annalise squeaked in her charming but high pitch voice.

As much as Alessandria loved her brother and his fiancé. She had to admit she had to deal with Annalise in small doses.

"Oh Alessandria, you must come shopping with us! It'll be a girls afternoon out!"

Alessandria would rather shoot herself!

Justin looked at her.

The Dominus Procurator gave Annalise a quick hug and said: "I'm afraid. I'm busy. I have a criminal to hunt down,"

"Oh that's okay. Come and meet us later!"

"Of course," Alessandria quickly started to walk away.

She didn't even have time to get to the market before Annalise squeaked. "Oh Alexis. Daniel wanted to see you,"

Alessandria paused. Why would her brother talk to Annalise?

He was autistic and hated talking to her with a passion. Talking to Annalise would be mental torture to him.

Alessandria stormed off to find a horse to find out what was so important.

CHAPTER 2

Gently pushing the hard brown wooden seat in from under me, I raised my head to look at the desk in front of me. I loved my desk.

Its hard black wooden features felt cold and smooth as I ran my fingers under it. Most people hated it. Saying it looked depressing and death like but I didn't care.

I guess that's a great benefit if being autistic. You don't overly care what people say. Despite my best efforts, and I promise you I do try, I just want people to go away. I tend to find people a bit much. There's was one boy who I liked to be around but that was a lifetime ago.

Lifting my fingers off the desk, I looked at the immense clock on the wall a few metres from me. The immense grandfather clock was... I don't know. I have no feelings towards it. It's a clock!

The same goes for the well vanished brown walls with their golden rims around me. I don't have feelings towards them. I known Alessandria liked them, but I ignored her.

Returning my attention to my desk, I picked up my long white quiver and tipped it in my... Ink pot.

I rolled my eyes. Someone had moved it a millimetre out of place for crying out loud. They moved it. Why. Why did they have to move it?

I took a few deep breaths, like my father had taught me before he was killed in the wars.

Shaking my head, I turned my head to start looking through the half a metre high pile of folders to my left. I smiled.

I loved being busy and productive. Definitely something I loved about autism was how productive it made me. For a so-called 'normal' person, it would take them a day or two to look through all those military contracts. Me, I'll be done in three hours.

Hearing heavy footsteps by the door and the disgusting smell of sweet perfumed oil filling the air, I played with my little blunt blade in my right hand to calm myself about the loud noise. I hated noise.

Continuing to turn the dull blade in my hand, I looked at the large golden door frame with its weird symbols and I saw a servant walk past.

I shook my head. Partly at the servant and partly at myself, don't get me wrong I love being autistic, but why did I have to get so stressed by the little things?

About to pick up my first folder, I heard a very quiet set of footsteps coming towards my office, I allowed a small smile to pass my lips.

"Alessandria, you can walk properly now,"

Her steps got louder.

I turned my dull blade quicker in my hand.

Alessandria carefully walked into the office wearing her, I suppose, *beautiful* long black cloak with the selves rolled up to show her tanned smooth skin.

Looking at her face, she gave a false smile at me. Her features were narrow but beautiful and her long blond hair flowed down her back.

She wanted to come closer and hug me but…

"I am sorry, Alessandria,"

"It's okay Daniel. I know hugging makes you uncomfortable,"

"I should thank you for trying. You seem to be the only one in his family who tries to respect me,"

"That's not true,"

A normal person might have laughed but I wasn't having any of it.

My dull blade turned quicker.

"Really?"

Yes, Daniel. Mother loves you and Justin loves you too,"

"Mother banishes me to this office, so she doesn't have to deal with me. Justin always tries to bring me outside. With all those people and the noise. The noise. The noise!"

My mind flooded with images of people in the streets shouting and screaming.

I stopped to take a few deep breaths.

Looking up at Alessandria, I thought I saw a tear in her eye. I knew she loved me. and I loved her in my own way. She was the only one besides father who ever tried.

"I am sorry," I said trying to relax. Banishing the thoughts of all those people and noise in the streets from my mind.

"It's okay, Daniel. And I know there's another reason why you can't be seen in public too much,"

I stared at her dead in the eye.

Before I remembered I hated eye contact and I looked at the ceiling.

"That is why I summoned you here,"

"You do not summon me, brother,"

"Oh sorry, I forget that's offensive. I asked… requested," I didn't know what's polite. "You here to ask you about what you knew about your brother's time as Dominus Procurator?"

"Our brother,"

I nodded.

He was no brother of mine as far as I'm concerned. A real brother would try to accommodate me in his life. Not make me feel like a convenience who's better off dead.

"I don't know much from when Justin was in my position. He only got promoted to Praetorian and being Mother's personal bodyguard last month. Then I got promoted from Procurator to Dominus Procurator,"

I simply nodded.

"Is there a case or something that you want me to relook? I've been busy learning about the other Procurators under me for the past month. I was going to start looking over the cases tomorrow,"

"No, thank you. I just wondered,"

"Daniel, your mind doesn't allow you to *just wonder*,"

Well, she knew me well.

"There is something you might find out when you start looking over the old cases. We need to talk when you come across it. Something about three years ago,"

She paused.

Her mouth started to open.

My arms started to burn.

"It's something I will not talk about. Three years ago was... a difficult time for me, Mother and Justin. You will learn about it in time, but I thought I would just warn you,"

I was lying, of course. I just wanted to know if she knew already. And yes, lying is bad so I hear. But lying serves a purpose.

Alessandria slowly nodded her head.

"Is that everything, Daniel?"

"Yes, Alessandria. I am sorry. It's seemed like I've wasted your time,"

"No problem at all. It's always nice seeing you. Will you join us for dinner tonight?"

Dinner!

I couldn't think of anything worse. All that small talk, the loud Annalise, no, no, no.

"No... I mean no thank you,"

Alessandria took a few steps closer to the desk.

"I am here for you if you ever need me,"

As much as she believed that, I knew it wasn't true. If that was true, she might have tried harder three years ago to figure out what was going on.

I gave her a sweet smile.

She started to walk out the door when she turned around and said: "I'm meant to be meeting Justin and Annalise for wedding shopping. I'll like you to join me if you want,"

I almost dropped my dull blade on the floor. This was the first time ever my sister had invited me out before.

But it was in the bust streets with people, loud people, and smelly people- and Annalise.

"You could get something for Geoff, and Hellen's coming too,"

Well, I guess I needed to get my husband-to-be something. I hated arranged marriages. Yet I do like Hellen.

Despite my better judgement, I forced out: "I... will come with you,"

CHAPTER 3

As her black leather boots pressed into the grey cobblestones of the road, Alessandria felt a small warmth pulse through her. Her boots gently tapped against the stone.

Looking ahead, Alessandria admired the tall shops with their wooden joints clear as day and their interesting choice of paint colour, either side of her. As she walked down the long road to the wedding shop at the bottom.

As she passed the pink cake shop to her left, she took a deep breath. Breathing in the delicious scents. With brilliant fruity, sweet tastes forming on her tongue. Was that honey and ginger?

Perhaps, she would have to find out later after this ordeal. She might have loved Justin. After all he was her older brother, the Family Praetorian and heir to the Noble House. But she had to make an effort to deal with Annalise.

In all honesty, she couldn't really understand why her mother had blessed the marriage. After her father died in the wars, control of the House went to Alessandria's mother and she was... particular about the future.

So, why she allowed Justin to marry a girl outside the nobility was beyond her.

Sure, Annalise came from a good family but considering her mother was scheming and cunning. Alessandria didn't see the point.

She shook her head. Trying to figure out her mother made her head hurt.

A tap of wood reminded Alessandria she wasn't alone.

Turning her head to the left, she saw Hellen wearing her long grey cloak as before. Carrying her wooden stick as she thumped it against the cobblestones.

Alessandria raised an eyebrow at the stick. She didn't think Hellen needed it to walk. They had both served in the military together and Hellen never needed any support. But Alessandria was curious to know why she carried it everywhere she went. What did the men she kept think of the stick?

She didn't want to know.

Speaking of men, Hellen looked to the right of the street as a young well muscular man walked past.

Alessandria had to admit the men was pleasing to look at but she wasn't going to stare. That wasn't what nobility did.

Despite that fact, she did catch Daniel giving the man a subtle stare. For some reason that made her happy. She knew Daniel's life wasn't easy and it was only in the past few months she had tried to be a sister to him. She hated herself for that but she was trying now.

Although, she could never understand why,

despite the afternoon sun still beaming down on them and Alessandria was sweating slightly, Daniel was wearing a long black leather cloak that went down to his knees with full length sleeves. That matched his black leather trousers and boots.

He must be boiling!

Anyway, the black made him look good with his strong jawline, blue eyes and brown hair brushed to the left.

Alessandria shook her head. Trying to clear her mind but she still couldn't understand Daniel's black leather cloak that stuck to his slim yet well-muscled figure.

In an attempt to break a silence that Alessandria did know was happening, Hellen questioned: "Why are we going to see ya brother? I had a criminal who needed to be taught a lesson back at the Justice Halls,"

Alessandria gave a little smile.

"Annalise wanted us to find some outfits for the wedding,"

"Dan, ya going to the wedding?" Hellen asked.

"I don't know. Probably. Yes, I will go. Geoff has been invited so I'll have to go,"

Alessandria had to admit it was nice seeing her brother and best friend talk as they passed yet another bakery on the street. Filling her senses with sticky sweet smells.

"Don't you want to go?" Alessandria asked.

"Not really. Why should I go through a day of pointless ceremony and boring speeches? When I could be doing something more productive that adds to the Kingdom and the House of Fireheart,"

Alessandria tried to answer but she hated it when her brother had good points.

"Dan look at it from my perspective, Justin and Annalise will be inviting all their rich and very attractive friends. Meaning I get a day of watching rich men in suits walking about and dancing in the evening. What's wrong with that?"

If the ground could swell Alessandria up, she would have wanted it to.

"As much as I would enjoy that. I still think my efforts and attention are better spent elsewhere,"

Alessandria looked to see how far the wedding shop was. It wasn't close enough.

"But a wedding tends to make people in the mood. Surely getting Geoff…"

"No more please, Hellen," Daniel snapped.

Alessandria turned to her brother and focused on the rapid turning off his dull blade in his hand. She always understood why he did it. Alessandria just didn't understand why talking about Geoff would annoy him.

Approaching the immense white shop front of the store, Alessandria took a deep breath to prepare herself. She walked up to the heavy iron cast door and she led everyone in.

Unlike a normal wedding shop, this store was dark with a row of small flickering candles around the edge of the textured ceiling.

In addition, to the dark cold oak floorboards where three mirrors arranged in a semi-circle laid in the middle of the chamber. With a rack of white dresses next to it.

Although, the semi-circle was arranged in a private way to hide the user trying on the dresses.

Additionally, there were four broken chairs to Alessandria's left as she entered the store.

All three of them walked in further.

"Something is wrong," Daniel plainly said.

"This isn't like any shop I've been to before," Hellen added.

"Alessandria," Daniel called.

Alessandria walked over to her brother who was by the rack of dresses. He pointed to a small pool of blood on the floor.

The Dominus Procurator's stomach flipped. Where was her brother?

"Alexis," Hellen quietly uttered.

Slowly, Alessandria and Daniel walked over to the semi-circle of mirrors.

Alessandria gasped.

Daniel smiled in shock.

In front of them was the stabbed corpse of Justin.

Ignoring the fact his brother was dead, Daniel knelt down next to the body.

Alessandria rolled her eyes and did the same. The cold floor pressing into her knees.

She had to admire her brother's taste in suits.

The tight, slightly shiny black suit with a white shirt looked good.

Daniel continued to check Justin's pockets.

"Simple murder really," Daniel plainly said.

A shot of rage built up inside Alessandria. She wanted to shout at her brother for his lack of decorum.

She wanted to hit him.

But her training kicked in.

She was Dominus Procurator of the House of Fireheart. Her brother was murdered. Her Family's Praetorian, Protector was dead.

Alessandria needed to find out who did this, and was someone trying to target her family?

"Oh, I'm sorry sister. The Corpse,"

Hellen placed a loving hand on his shoulder.

Daniel tensed even more than usual but he relaxed.

Alessandria smiled.

"I'll do the talking, Danny,"

"Do not call me that,"

She ignored him.

"Clear and effective. A single thrust of a narrow blade through the heart. Simple way but always effective," Hellen explained.

Daniel stood up and walked away.

Alessandria didn't give him much thought.

"But how did something get the jump on Justin? Me, Daniel, and Justin all had to serve at least six months in the military. Justin served two years. It doesn't make sense,"

"Alessandria," Daniel plainly spoke.

She rolled her eyes and walked a few metres away to find Daniel standing by a wooden doorframe that presumably led to the back stores.

He pointed down to the floor below.

Alessandria gave a little smile as she saw Annalise's dead body. Again, a single stab wound through the heart.

Leading Daniel and Hellen to the other side of the semi-circle of mirrors so she didn't have to look at the bodies anymore. Alessandria started: "Hellen, go to the Castle please and get more Procurators. Me and…"

The window smashed.

A metal can hit the floor.

Thick smoke filled the shop.

Everyone coughed.

Alessandria saw Daniel tense.

A man stormed through the shop door. Gun raised.

CHAPTER 4

As the smoke filled the shop, I wanted to scream. I wanted to lash out. The noise, the noise, the noise of the smashing glass raining down on the wooden floor was horrible.

My throat was clogged with thick black smoke.

In my hand, the dull blade turned quickly and quicker as I tried to calm myself.

I needed to fight back the urge to scream.

The smoke started to clear.

My throat was starting to ease as a man exploded through the door with his gun raised. He stared at us.

Then my beautiful autistic mind kicked in, this man was tall with a thick brown beard and disgusting messy hair, not my type.

Although, his brutish features were interesting. Along with his padded blue robes and fiery red armour piqued my interest.

I looked over to Helen, who probably wanted to thump him and Alessandria who… I don't know what she wanted to do.

Returning my limited attention back to this man, my eyes narrowed on his gun. It was grey with golden highlights and spots of blood on the barrel. High quality, well made.

Certainly wouldn't have come from the street or Noble Houses. Definitely the Queen or… another possibility that I didn't want to entertain.

Regardless of who this man belonged to, he had no right to bust in there. I'm aware of no social rule that allows it, but this is hardly my area of expertise.

With the smoke clearing, I started to detect a disgusting hint of clove and other spices. I would have liked to know what a 'normal' person would have thought of the smell, but this was hardly the time.

The man took a step towards me, Alessandria looked at me with harsh eyes.

She knew I would attack if the man did a wrong move. Since I have extreme reflexes and extreme protective instincts.

"By Order of the House of Fireheart, identify yourself!" Alessandria ordered.

I thought it was a bit dramatic but that's why I'm not the Dominicus Procurator.

The man sneered at Alessandria.

I wanted, I needed to punch him.

"You have no authority over me, woman. I am an Inquisitor of the Queen's Holy Inquisition and you are all under arrest,"

I busted out laughing.

Of all the Queen's organisations, why did the Inquisition have to turn up?

These self-righteous idiots who think themselves gods.

Of course, they might only answer to the Queen, but these Inquisitors are horrid arrogant people. I would rather shoot myself than work with one.

I decided to walk away and focus on Justin's body.

With my footsteps tapping against the wooden floor, I heard the Inquisitor roar behind me: "Where is he going!"

I felt a hand grab me.

A hand!

Someone touched me!

No!

I swung around.

I didn't think.

No one touches me.

I grabbed the hand.

Sinking my long nails into his flesh.

I felt warm blood go up my arm.

I smiled.

My fists raised to punch him. Then Alessandria grabbed me from behind.

I kept screaming.

People kept touching me.

"NO!" I screamed.

Alessandria spun me around and hugged me. She took long deep breaths so I would copy her and relax.

"He touched me," I whispered.

In my ear she whispered, "I know. You're safe,"

She gave me a quick kiss on the head before I pushed away. Snarling at the Inquisitor as I stood behind Hellen.

Like she would be able to protect me.

The Inquisitor stared at with hate and rage as he wiped the large scratch marks clean from blood.

"Inquisitor, I would stop staring at my brother if I were you. Too much eye contact is bad for you as well,"

"That freak! I'll have him arrested and killed for attacking an Inquisitor,"

I wanted to storm forward and finish the job, but Alessandria raised a hand before I could move.

"You shall do no such thing, Inquisitor. I am in charge of this crime scene and this is my investigator, and as for my brother... he will not be going anywhere,"

"The Procurators be of the Queen or the vile Nobility has no power over me. Now move aside!"

"Inquisitor, what Order are you from? The Blessed Earth? Holy Water? Divine Air? Gifted Metal?"

"Ha! Those Orders are weak. I am from the Order of the Sacred Fire,"

My heart sank. Of all the Inquisitors to meet, why did it have to be an Inquisitor from a hardcore extremist Order?

In all honesty, he probably wanted to kill Hellen right now because she showed a piece of skin where the cloak opened slightly. And as for me, I really didn't want him to know I was gay.

I noticed even Alessandria was a bit taken by the identification of his Order.

"Inquisitor, do you have a name? I am..."

"I know who you are, Alessandria Fireheart. It is your family who is corrupting the mortal fabric of this country!"

Oh god, he's one of those idiots.

Now, I didn't drink but I see the temptation in moments like this.

"Okay, what is your name?"

"I am Inquisitor Nemesio of…"

I was growing bored of this man.

"Good for you. Why are you here Nemesis?" I asked.

"Nemesio! Are you dyslexia too! I am here because my Order got a tip that you three were killing innocent people,"

"A bit harsh and no I'm no dyslexic. And it's a shame to see the mighty Orders relying on tips now. I remember when the Orders were all-powerful with agents on every corner. How far the mighty fall,"

Hellen playfully tapped my legs with her stick.

"My brother makes a good point, in his own way. We only just arrived, and we were upset. Look around all you want Nemesio, you'll find two bodies. Both with single stab wounds to the heart. I must leave you to start my own investigations,"

With that, Alessandria started to walk out. Hellen and I quickly followed.

Just as we reached the door, Nemesio shouted: "You nobility are a disgrace and I will prove you killed your brother and his wife,"

Alessandria continued to walk out before she stopped. She turned around and passed me as she went to stood right next to the Inquisitor.

Personally, I wouldn't have wanted to stand anywhere near him. She was brave, I'll give her that.

"If you want to monitor me and my House. You can always join us and do a joint investigation. I can promise you; your life will be easier that way,"

He paused.

"Are you threatening an Inquisitor! I could have your entire House burned to the ground in a second,"

Alessandria rolled her eyes.

"But I will join you. At least, I can get proof on how you're corrupting the moral fabric of our society. But know this Dominicus Procurator if I find evidence of your crimes. All of you will die!"

CHAPTER 5

Passing a black tie servant as she walked in, Alessandria and the Inquisitor entered her Mother's office.

Alessandria shook her head as she could still see and hear Nemeiso moaning and condemning her as he hated the rest of the castle.

She couldn't understand what he hated about it. The rose gardens were perfectly clean and beautiful as was the apple orchard and the other fruit trees and bushes.

The castle itself was a stunning blend of practical and impenetrable granite and beautiful marble. And that was before you considered the stunning murals of battles and ancient relics that lived inside the castle.

Alessandria supposed he could be moaning about the young servants but they were paid three times the legal minimum wage and everyone was equal here. Then Alessandria remembered that the Inquisitor was a foul moany man anyway.

No wonder Daniel had run to his room and Hellen had escaped as soon as she left the shop. To get other Procurators to bring the bodies back to the castle for examination.

Turning her attention back to the present, Alessandria wondered through her mother's mighty office and despite her visiting here hundreds, if not thousands of times, she still loved it.

The immense circular office with shelves upon shelves of ancient leather books and folders to your left. Then rows upon rows of ancient and mystical objects from by gone eras and father's travels. It was a paradise for the mind.

Alessandria looked up at the golden domed ceiling to see the evening sky dazzle through the glass.

Nemesio's heavy footsteps banging against the polished concrete filled the office to Alessandria's annoyance.

As the two investigators got to the middle of the office, Alessandria noticed the Inquisitor looking and studying the blue circular patterns on the floor. She understood why he was interested. They were stunning in their complexity.

Casting her mind back, Alessandria remembered her father had said they were something to do with the Empire before Ordericous and the founding of the Inquisitorial Orders.

Looking away from the Inquisitor, Alessandria kept walking. Feeling the warm air, from mother's small fire on the far side of the Office, washing over her face.

In addition, to the wine scented candles, her mother was burning. Or as Alessandria liked to phrase it, the wine her mother spilt and decided to light it.

As Alessandria and Nemesio approached the immense brown wooden desk, that weighted over ten tonnes and at least three metres in width with piles of maps and folders on there, a woman raised her empty wine glass on them.

Alessandria had to admire her mother's style. Despite, the chaos of maps and folders around her, she still caught your eye. With her long elegant white dress and silver, blond long hair. Even her golden necklace highlighted her well-aged features. Making her look young. Then there was the typical wine glass in her right hand, or sometimes both.

As Alessandria approached her, her mother poured herself another massive glass of black wine. Finishing the bottle.

"Alexis darling, you didn't tell me you were bringing company! Oh, he's fabulous. Strong, fit. What noble family is he from?"

"I am not from your disgusting nobility!"

Alessandria's mother downed her wine and stood up.

"Listen here mister, I am Lady Kinaaz of the House of Fireheart. You do not disrespect me in my own castle,"

Knowing the Inquisitor was about to make things worse, Alessandria jumped in: "Mother, this is Inquisitor Nemesio of the Order of the Sacred Fire,"

"I could have guessed that. You do not get to be in my position without knowing how to spot an Inquisitor,"

"I knew it. Your family is guilty!"

Kinaaz cocked her head and looked around for another bottle.

"Mother, he is here to investigate… Mum you might want to sit down,"

"Your son is dead. He was murdered," Nemesio added.

Kinaaz fell to the floor.

Whacking her head on the desk.

Her blood dripped onto the floor.

Alessandria rushed over to her mother and held her as her mother cried.

Alessandria wanted nothing more than to rip Nemesio's throat out. Even Daniel wouldn't have been that callous. What's worse is, unlike Daniel, this Inquisitor knew it was wrong to shout that out!

After a few moments, Kinaaz weakly placed her hands on Alessandria's face.

"Is Justin dead?"

"Yes, and Annalise,"

Kinaaz pushed herself up, brushed herself off and sat back on her chair.

"That's not good. With Justin dead that is… I need time to think,"

Alessandria shook her head in disbelief. She knew her mother had at times seem cold and distant since her father died. But her mother wasn't this callous, was she?

"Lady Kinaaz, you will answer my questions!"

"Oh what! My son is dead, and my family is in danger. I need to protect my last two children!"

"Mother as Dominicus Procurator leave that to me. I'll…"

Nemesio coughed.

"*We'll* find out what happened. Have you or Justin received any threats lately?"

Kinaaz busted out laughing.

"Honey, honey, honey when you're Lady Fireheart. You'll receive death threats every minute or every day. Especially, when you're as liberal as us,"

"Okay, but what do you mean when I'm Lady Fireheart? With Justin dead, Daniel is surely the next Heir. He's the best person for the job. He runs our military and weapons operations,"

Kinaaz looked at Alessandria.

"Inquisitor please give us a moment,"

"Don't be so stupid. I will not be leaving your disgraceful sides until my investigation is done,"

"Fine. Alexis, yes Daniel will make a great Lord Fireheart one day. But... he can never be Lord Fireheart. Because he's...well... gay,"

Kinaaz looked around for the wine bottle again.

"Wait! Abortion, gay marriage, gay adoption, everything is legal in this country because of us and other noble houses but a gay person becoming the head of a Noble House is illegal!"

Her mother searched for that bottle of wine.

"Alessandria that is the way it must be. This country has already been degraded enough..." Nemesio stated coldly.

"Don't you dare speak to me! This is your doing," Alessandria turned back to her mother who was drinking heavily from a wine bottle. "I do not want to be Lady Fireheart when you die. I am to be a Dominicus Procurator in the field, solving crime for the rest of my life,"

Her mother finished the bottle.

"Alexis, I love you, but you need to grow up. Daniel will never be Lord Fireheart unless there's a law change. So please grow up and start acting like a future Lady,"

Alessandria started to shake.

Tears began to feel her eyes.

For the first time ever, she realised her life wasn't her own to lead. She was a puppet for the Nobility.

Alessandria stormed off.

Nemesio followed and grabbed her by the arm.

Out of the corner of her eye, Alessandria saw her mother preparing to throw a wine bottle at him,

"Storm off all you want but I am coming too. As for your law change idea, I know you want it. But the Inquisition will never allow it,"

"Then I will kill you all in the end but I am not becoming Lady Fireheart,"

CHAPTER 6

Allowing the soft warm black silk covers to touch my skin, I laid on my bed with my leathered booted feet in the air. My dull blade was spinning fast in my hand as I tried to forget about that Inquisitor.

I was too rageful to rant or curse my feelings about him so I forced myself to focus on my bedroom.

But he touched me!

Taking another breath and spinning my dull blade as fast as I could in my hand. (I understand why father dulled it for me. But I much preferred the blade when it was sharp!) I focused on my room.

This was my space and no one was allowed inside except another servant that was gay to do the cleaning. He was nice to talk to from time to time but I always hoped he wasn't in here whenever I came back to my room. I didn't want to be around people. This was my room. A place for me to relax and 'centre' myself when the world got a bit much.

Anyway, I turned my head to the left to admire my massive brown chest of draws with various notebooks and blades on the top. In front of a large window that allowed the evening light to shine in and the moon rise.

You might think it weird, me having a collection of blades but I like sharp objects and military history. The stories some of those blades could tell from thousands of years ago in far away lands.

As I turned my head to the other side of the room, seeing the plain stone ceiling as I turned, to see the heavy oak door out of the corner of my eye. In addition, to the tall and thick black metal wardrobe.

I didn't know why I was made to have it so big. I practically live in my black leather cloak and trousers. Anything that covers up my arms.

My dull blade started to slow in my hand as I relaxed and I turned onto my stomach. Resting my head into the big black velvet pillows.

They didn't smell of much, thankfully but I liked that. I hated strong smells. I hated... I just wanted to sleep. Yet going to sleep would involve me lifting up my weighted covers. I couldn't be asked with that.

And it's not weird I need weighted covers but I like the feeling of having something pressed against me. I started to feel my eyelids starting to get heavy.

My door exploded open.

Someone walked in.

I grabbed the knife under my pillow.

Jumped up on the bed and I went to jump. Then I saw it was Alessandria.

She stared at me in confusion, and she wiped a few more tears from her eyes. I hate it when they cry. I don't know how to deal with them.

Then that stupid Inquisitor walked in behind

my sister. I rolled my eyes and laid back on my bed. I really didn't care for Inquisitor Nemesio at this moment.

My back started to warm up as I felt the Inquisitor's piecing glaze stare with hate at me.

Just to be nice, I decided to ask: "Are you okay, Alessandria?"

I partially cared but the Inquisitor was dampening my mood.

"Did you know you couldn't be Lord Fireheart?"

She knew!

Forcing myself up, I climbed over the bed and sat on the edge closest to her. I gestured I was going to hold her hand, but I couldn't bring myself to touch her.

"Yes, I knew. I have to deal with all our military and weapon contracts. I know a good 90% of our laws. I've known for years as did father,"

Now, I'm not very good at reading facial expressions but I think she's making a sad face with a hint of anger.

"The law's wrong. I can't run a Noble House. I can't look after our House and Our people,"

"Not with that attitude," I said.

"Are you okay with this?"

Before I could answer, Nemesio added: "It does not matter what he thinks. The Law is the Law. You and your liberal allies have done enough damage to us,"

I looked over my shoulder. Eyeing up each and every one of my blades. Wondering which one would be best to cut out his throat with. I hardly had a lack of choices.

Alessandria cleared her throat.

"Alessandria, I am fine with these stupid laws," then I looked at the Inquisitor, knowing his reaction. "I can marry whatever man I wanted. I can raise children and hold a man's hand in public. So I am fine about not being Lord Fireheart,"

As I predicted, I knew the Inquisitor would stare at me with hateful eyes and his hands formed fists. If I wanted to really annoying, I could blow him a false kiss but I have standards.

"Alessandria are you here for a particular reason?"

She cocked her head at me.

"Our brother is dead. I came to see if you're okay,"

I forget when someone dies, you're meant to be sad.

Trying to fake cry, I tried to force a tear out but I almost looked as if I was mocking my sister by accident.

"I'm sorry. I am not mocking you. I can't cry over my brother's death,"

"You did it!" the Inquisitor screamed. "You killed your brother,"

I looked at Alessandria in confusion. Even her eyes widened at the craziness of that idea.

"He did no such thing," she firmly said.

"You nobility might be able to fool others, but my eyes are clear. Daniel Fireheart I am arresting you,"

He came for me.

He grabbed one of my leather sleeves.

I jumped away. I couldn't move.

He touched me!

He touched!

I jumped away.

My leather cloak ripped.

As I jumped across the bed, Nemesio grabbed my other sleeve.

Pulling it.

The sleeve ripped again.

Relieving my arms.

Alessandria gave a quiet scream.

The Inquisitor stopped and stared at my arms.

Looking down at my arms, I saw the 3-year-old deep red cuts with circular patterns all over my arms. I still remember the blade dripping with my blood. I ran my fingers over the scars. Feeling their cold painful marks on my skin.

The Inquisitor took a step toward me.

I screamed.

I dived for him.

Alessandria grabbed me from behind.

I kicked her and scratched her.

"Get out!" she screamed at the Inquisitor.

I kept kicking. Feeling my powerful legs hit

Alessandria's multiple times.

Three black armoured women with spears and rifles came to the door to escort the Inquisitor out of the castle.

One of the women shut the wooden door behind them. Alessandria threw me on to the bed.

I grabbed the weighted black bed sheet and pulled it over me.

"I'm sorry," I shouted through the material.

Hearing Alessandria rubbing her legs, I had to smile slightly not from being proud but... it was my way of coping.

"I know Daniel. I'm sorry for bringing him in here,"

"Are you okay about the Lord Fireheart thing?"

Well, I had to ask. I did injure her after all.

"I will change the law, Daniel. You will be Lord Fireheart,"

"Why don't you want to be Lady Fireheart?"

"Because Daniel, I don't want to have to deal with everything. I don't want to be tied to the House. I want to be out in the world investigating and solving crimes,"

"I can understand that. Why did you come here in the first place?"

Whilst she tried to remember, my body relaxed, and I smiled as the weight of the bedsheet pressed on me. There was something calming in that.

"Oh, the investigation has stalled. There are

no witnesses or fingerprints at the crime scene. Tomorrow, I'll have to start going through the death threats and finding leads there,"

"What about Annalise? She was in a hiding position. She might have seen the attackers,"

"What? You want to use your Flesheater ability to try and see if you can identify the killers using her flesh memories?"

"It's worth a try. We'll all lesser magic users in our family,"

"I'll talk to the Inquisitor in a moment. I'll see if he can bring us some flesh samples tomorrow morning,"

"Thank you," I replied and thought I'll be nice by asking: "Are you okay about Justin? I think you two were close?"

I heard her give a slight laugh. "Yes, me and him were close. When I got back from my 6 months in the military, he made me a Procurator and he trained me to become Dominus. He was great as a friend and a brother,"

Inside my bedsheet fort, I rolled my eyes at the thought of Justin being a good brother. So, I had to say something.

Poking my arm out, and being slightly shocked at the temperature difference, I said: "Alexis, these marks. You'll learn what happened one day, but do you know what Justin said to me when he found my bleeding body,"

I heard her move uncomfortably.

"What?"

"He said: *the useless idiot finally did it*," I paused for dramatic effect and I remembered the rage and upset that my barely conscious body felt. "Then I heard mother come in and raise the alarm. She is what saved me. So forgive me if I am not upset that my brother is dead,"

CHAPTER 7

As the wind blew the rows upon rows of red, golden and purple roses flapped ever so slightly. Releasing sweet perfume into the air.

Alessandria breathed in deeply if only for a moment of calm before her day started. She looked around the rose gardens quickly. Admiring all of its hundred metres of pure natural beauty. From the perfectly straight rows of roses to the interesting shapes of the oyster shells that were used as a border around the beds.

Taking a step further into the rose garden, Alessandria felt the wet morning dew chill her boots. Sending cold pulses through her foot.

She could understand why Daniel loved the morning. Especially, on a cold winter's day. It was the middle of summer now but she still understood.

Casting her mind back to last night, she had paced for two hours after leaving Daniel. She really didn't want to leave him, especially with his blade collection, but she had dealt with self-harming people as a Procurator and she found the more you fussed the worse it got, to a point.

Alessandria was still pretty shaken by it though. How could Justin be so heartless?

Why didn't he try to get help?

Yet she had to admit what was concerning her more was where was she during all of this?

Rubbing her forehead, Alessandria tried to remember but three years ago was drawing a blank. She could remember her first kill, military tour and her first criminal but three years ago was a blank.

Turning her attention back to the rose garden, Alessandria beamed a little as she saw Daniel walk towards her. Wearing his typical black leather cloak and trousers. She wondered how many black cloaks does he have?

Daniel slowly spun his dull blade in his hand and nodded to his sister.

Alessandria released a little breath at knowing Daniel was still talking to her and wasn't acting weird... Or any more weird after last night.

The sound of marching footsteps caused Alessandria to turn to her left. To see three fully armed black armoured men escorting the Inquisitor in his fiery red armour towards them.

The Dominicus Procurator looked at Nemesio and gave a small evil grin as she saw two small jars filled with red stuff in his left hand.

She had to admit of all the Lesser Magical Users in the world. Daniel certainly had the most interesting. Being able to see and feel what someone saw as they were dying was interesting to say the least.

The Inquisitor gave Daniel a small snarl as he greeted Alessandria and passed her the small jars.

Alessandria held the jars up to the bright

sunlight above them. Allowing the blood red brain matter to sparkle in the light.

"Thank you, Inquisitor. I am a bit surprised you agreed to such a thing," Alessandria said matter-of-factly.

"The Orders have no problem using magic. It is the end that justifies the means. Even if we have to deal with his kind of people,"

Daniel smiled a little at the comment and Alessandria had to agree with him. This was petty even for an Inquisitor.

"Tell me, Noble filth. How does this work?"

Knowing Daniel was going to ignore him, Alessandria explained. "It's simple really. My brother will eat these chunks of brain and then, for lack of a better term, he'll see what Justin and Annalise saw,"

Nemesio rolled his eyes.

"That sounds disgusting and vile,"

Alessandria felt a wave of coldness pulse through her.

"Now, now Inquisitor that's a lie. You're interested in this,"

Nemesio's eyes widened slightly. His hand started to go for a blade.

The three armed men went for the Inquisitor.

Alessandria waved them to stop.

"Inquisitor, each of my member is a Lesser Magic User. My brother a Flesheater. Me, a True Seer. Do not lie to me,"

Nemesio rolled his eyes.

"Let us be done with this, abominations!"

Alessandria gave a light chuckle and threw Daniel the jar labelled Justin.

He caught it, popped the cork, and looked at

it.

"Come on, Daniel. I know you don't eat meat but come on,"

Daniel frowned and swirled it.

"Come on do it for the family,"

"You're loving this, aren't you?"

"It's your face I'm laughing at,"

Daniel raised the jar to his lips, and he threw the brain matter down in one mouthful.

He coughed.

Slowly, magical energy crackled around him and Daniel's eyes turned bright white.

Alessandria simply stared at her brother as his eyes flashed and his mouth moved in strange foreign languages.

Daniel's dull blade fell from his hand as his body moved and jerked.

After a few seconds, his eyes returned to normal. He picked up his dull blade.

"So freak, what did you see?"

Alessandria nodded him to answer.

"Justin saw nothing but… he only felt the blade piece his heart. He was too deep in thought to hear the people come in,"

"People?" Alessandria asked.

"Yes, it was outside his conscious awareness. But he heard two sets of footsteps. As he died, he screamed out a message,"

"What message?"

"Just the typical loving stuff. Like *Annalise*!"

Alessandria felt a wave of coldness pulse through her. Why did Daniel lie?"

Looking at the other jar, Alessandria hoped Annalise's brain would provide something more useful. She threw it at Daniel. He downed it.

Magic crackled around him and the process happened again.

After a minute, Daniel returned, and he fell to the ground gasping.

Alessandria walked over and offered him a hand. He refused.

"Speak, freak,"

"Annalise saw the attackers. There were two of them. Two men dressed in common white tunics. They were effective. They walked in and stabbed them both within seconds,"

"Anything more specific? A facial feature that was unique to them?"

"Yes, the taller man. He had a crescent-shaped scar around his right eye,"

"Was it infected? A slight greenish-blue colour?"

"Do you know something, woman?" Nemesio pressed.

"Yes, I know who the killers are, but I'm afraid they're hired guns. This investigation is far from over,"

CHAPTER 8

As myself, the jerk of the Inquisitor and Alessandria stood outside a small dirty yellow house with a broken wooden door and cracked glass windows, I constantly drank water. Trying to clear the disgusting taste of brain from my mouth.

The worst thing was I would be walking or riding the horse to this house, move my tongue and my tongue would catch a bit of brain in between my teeth, and I would get random flashbacks. It was so annoying!

Alessandria kept staring at me. I knew she was laughing at me and I just have been pulling some strange faces but brain matter tastes disgusting!

This Flesheater ability is a curse too. It's why I can't eat meat. Which is a shame considering before these powers manifested I really liked bacon!

With a final swirl of water around my mouth, I cleaned it. Allowing us to enter the house.

Normally, we would have walked in with our swords but we knew the two criminals weren't home yet.

Personally, I was surprised Alessandria knew

who they were and she mentioned that Justin, curse that name, had been investigating them for possible organised crime. I couldn't care less what these people did, but they needed dealing with.

Now, I suggested we tortured them and stuck red hot metal in them, but Alessandria said that was extreme and unneeded.

The more horrific thing was the Inquisitor agreed with me- the so-called freak.

As we entered the house, I had to give a small chuckle at the disgrace of the place. Now, I'm not a gay who's into interior design but the house was only one dark room with two cracked windows either side of the door, two straw beds that looked like rats called them home and a small brown table without chairs.

This was hardly a home but it proved a point. These criminals barely spend time here. I understand why. It's disgusting!

I followed Alessandria over to the table in the middle of the house. We both ran our fingers across it. Feeling the rough wood with a thick layer of dust. What was the point of this place?

With the moving of the rats becoming louder, we all moved over to a pile of straw on the right side of the house. To see tens of rats moving in amongst the straw.

Again, this was wrong and unneeded.

The Inquisitor took out some matches from his red fiery armour and lit them. Burning the straw and rats in the process. It certainly warned the room up.

Thankfully, the squeaking of the rats and the thin grey smoke didn't draw too much attention to us.

"There's nothing here," the Inquisitor pointlessly said.

"I didn't expect to find much. These two aren't exactly of low intelligence,"

"How do you know them, Alessandria?" I asked, not sure if I was actually interested.

"I suspected them of being a part of a gang that operates on the House of Greenscales' land. But they're started to conduct their business on our soil,"

I was right. I wasn't interested.

"There must be something here!" Nemesio ordered.

Looking carefully around the room, I have to agree with the horrible thing of a man. In the far corner, where the wall met the floor. There was a budging piece of wood.

Walking over to it, I kicked the wood hard. It broke. Revealing a few sheets of paper. Since they were covered in stinking rat liquid, I quickly passed them to the Inquisitor.

Well, I was to give them to Alessandria. I did like her.

I heard a noise outside.

Alessandria heard it too and walked over to the door.

Two men walked in.

One tall overweight man stunk of dirty oil, wearing a dirty black tunic, stared at Alessandria.

The other thin man wearing a moderately expensive suit stared with rageful hate at Nemesio.

Nemesio charged.

The two men whipped out large knives.

Alessandria charged the larger man.

I stood there in the background. Waiting for

my time to strike.

The thin man hit punched Nemesio in the jaw.

The Inquisitor kicked him in the chest.

Alessandria whipped out her long red sword and swung in at the large man.

She wasn't kidding around.

Alessandria chopped off the larger man's knife wielding hand.

I ran over. Picking up the knife.

The larger man went to attack Alessandria.

I slid under his legs, jumped up and thrusted the blade into the back of his head.

The larger man fell to the floor.

Blood gushing out of the wound.

I heard a scream.

We turned around to see the thinner man in a headlock by Nemesio.

Looking back at the body, I had to admit I did like the odd kill from time to time. Only for those who deserve death. But it certainly made you feel alive in a fight.

"Release him Inquisitor," Alessandria ordered.

The Inquisitor tightened his grip.

The thinner man gagged.

"Why did you kill Justin Fireheart?" Alessandria questioned.

The man wouldn't speak.

"Who hired you!" the Inquisitor shouted.

"He will not speak. The gangs have too much of an honour code for that," I explained with boredom.

Knowing I had better things to do, I wandered over to the man and I begrudgingly knew exactly how to speed this along.

Staring at the man, I wondered what he had done in his futile life.

I decided to find out.

Whipping out my knife, I sliced off his ear.

Before I could change my mind, I ate it.

As the magical energy crackled around me, I heard Alessandria gave a shocked gasp and a snarl from the Inquisitor.

My vision blurred and I kept repeating Justin's awful name in my mind. Forcing the Flesheater power to find something to do with him.

Of course, it's easier to use the Flesheater ability on brain matter but I couldn't eat meat. So, the same idea applies.

Images of coins changing hands and a drawing of Justin and Annalise filled my mind.

It was dark and chaotic.

There was a man giving the killer the orders.

Great flashes of rage came from the speaker.

I couldn't see him. He was wearing a brown cloak.

Yet there was a golden ring with a weird symbol.

Certainly a man from a Noble House.

No, no, not the emotions. The sounds. The lights.

It's too much!

Through my sheer force of Will, I screamed free of these Flesh Memories.

When my vision focused, I found myself in Alessandria's arms and the Inquisitor staring at me.

"What did you see, brother?"

"It's someone from a Noble House. I couldn't

see which one,"

"Just typical. The Nobility breaking laws and killing people again. You're probably lying about the fact you didn't see the House. No matter, I'll just order you all be rounded up and tortured for information,"

Nemesio started to walk out of the house.

"The party tonight," I whispered, still feeling weak and overstimulated.

Alessandria rolled her eyes at forgetting about the awful occasion and then she dropped me.

My head hitting the cold dirty floor.

Thanks!

"Inquisitor, there's a party tonight at the House of Fireheart. It's meant to be for Justin's and Annalise's engagement. But Mother is insisting it still goes ahead. The entire Nobility of Ordericous will be there. You could subtly ask questions there. I'll be investigating,"

Still lying on the floor, I saw the Inquisitor snarled and his hands form fists in frustration.

"Fine. I will go to your stupid party. At least, I can get more evidence on the corruption of the Nobility,"

CHAPTER 9

Taking off her pure white corset, allowing the reasonably cold air of her bed chamber to touch her tanned skin. Alessandria ran her fingers over the fine blue, purple and red silk dresses a maid had picked for her. That hung over a black flowery cover?

Yet she couldn't consider what she would wear for this silly occasion.

As the Dominicus Procurator, she had advised her mother to cancel the party. Then Kinaaz had thrown a freshly finished wine bottle at her.

Alessandria really didn't understand why her mother was so determined to have this party. The party meant to celebrate the engagement or the fact Justin had picked a wedding date. With him dead it was so pointless!

At least Alessandria now understood why Daniel had tried so hard to escape it.

She gave a short laugh.

Kneeling down to take her boots off, she felt the cold floor press into her knees. She rolled her eyes at the thought of the maids not putting on the heating for the guests.

The last thing Alessandria needed was to give the nobility another reason to hate her family.

Slipping off her boots, Alessandria popped her head out from the covers to see Hellen enjoying her bed. Her stick was leaning against the cream stone walls. Whilst Hellen was cuddling into Alessandria's extremely soft blue sheets and firm supportive mattress.

She wouldn't have minded Hellen treating herself to the noble luxuries. But the more she moved the more the lavender in the sheets got released.

She hated the smell of lavender!

Then there was the fact Hellen wasn't exactly wearing anything appropriate for a noble party.

Although that wasn't entirely her fault as Alessandria remembered the time when her mother had thrown a whole glass of wine at Hellen's only good dress. That was years ago now but it still made them both laugh.

Returning her attention to picking out a dress, Alessandria traced her fingers across a blood red silk dress that would cover up most of her body.

Under normal conditions, she would think she looked like a tomato but at least the other nobles would know she was hunting tonight.

"Aren't ya done yet?" Hellen shouted from the bed.

Alessandria really didn't need her friend being impatient.

"No. I got a maid to get you a dress. She'll be here soon,"

"I don't need a dress. I'm fine as I am,"

"You're wearing your grey cloak and black

Procurator Armour. That's not okay for a noble party!"

"Oh I don't know. I think some of ya peers are shady,"

Alessandria threw her hands in the air.

"I think that's the point of a nobility,"

"Are you the only House that doesn't have an illegal side business?"

"Pretty much, the Greenscales are pretty clean. They sometimes grow weed on their land but that's about it,"

"Ah, has ya House ever committed a crime?"

"You sound like a Dominicus Procurator in the making,"

"Ha. That's no fun. Anyway, who's that boy on the stairs when we came up?"

Really, her best friend had been here for two hours and she was ready hunting for her next adventure.

"Short boy, young in black suit and tie?"

"Yea, that one,"

"Believe in or not, he's an Emissary from the Church,"

"What?"

"I know after the Church publicly declared us: *tainted* because we allowed Daniel to stay in the family. They haven't spoken to us,"

"Why he's here then?"

"I think Mother wants them to do Justin's burial,"

"Pointless, just dig a hole, put him in and say a few magical words,"

"Ha, no wonder you and Daniel get on so well,"

Alessandria took the red silk dress off her cover and held it over herself.

She had to admit the dress felt nice and smooth, and it certainly highlighted areas of herself. Perfect for a Noble party but it did smell a bit.

"When the maid comes remind me to ask for some strong perfume!"

"Yea," Hellen said as she presumably went back to enjoying the bed sheets. "Oh, I forgot to mention, the report came back on those papers Daniel found in that house!"

"Oh, what did they say?"

"Not a lot. But there is another name on the documents. Seems to be someone they wanted to talk to,"

"What name?" Alessandria asked as she considered the pair of earrings she was going to wear.

She picked up the dress so she could start to put it on.

"Someone called Harrison Gearing,"

Alessandria dropped the dress and knocked over her leather boots.

"You okay back there?"

"Yes, thank you. That's a name I haven't heard for ages. I'll get Daniel to go and see him. It'll be good for him to see an old friend,"

"Old friend, where they close? Boyfriends?"

"Yes, they were close. Mother hated Harrison. I liked him. I know Daniel had a crush on him, but he was straight,"

"Hasn't Daniel seen him for a while?"

"No, not for probably 3 years…" Alessandria started before the other words died in her mouth. She didn't know how she thought the two were connected, but her Procurator instincts told her they were. She would have to ask Daniel about that boy later.

A series of immense bangs came from the wooden door in front of the covers.

"Hel get the door. It's the maid. Get dressed and ask the maid for my perfume!" Alessandria shouted through her silk dress. Wanting to get to the party and find out who murdered her brother.

CHAPTER 10

My heart started to pump a little faster as I, with Alessandria attached to my right arm, entered the immense ballroom of our castle. The room was certainly pleasant with its smooth domed wall and ceilings. With the oversized chandelier hanging from the ceiling. Allowing the ballroom to be perfectly illuminated.

Despite being autistic I have to admit, I do rather enjoy parties. Granted I hate the music, people, talking and everything because it is a bit much for me. What I like about parties are the opportunities you can find. From forging alliances to making alliances of a more primal nature, parties can offer you everything.

Also, whilst this party might be in mine and his soon to be husband's honour, I had absolutely no intention of being here for too long.

Anything to get away from Geoff, I know mother honestly arranged the whole marriage out of love, but I hated it. Plus, it really annoyed me that he wasn't even gay!

Anyway, returning my attention to the party, me and Alessandria walked elegantly through the immense ballroom. We were both looking at the things-the guests. For the entire nobility was here from all the four Lords and Mother to all their children. And I definitely admit the nobility knows how to produce good looking men.

Presumably from the way Hellen was looking walking around and talking to everyone, she had realised that fact too.

As we passed waiters and waitresses in their posh black and white suits, my senses were filled with the delicious smells of sweet juicy fruits and rich meats. Then I smelt the more disgusting scents of alcohol and gin as Alessandria grabbed one of the long clear glasses filled with bubbling spirits.

I shook my head as a waiter offered me a glass.

Continuing to watch the nobility, they were all on the edges of the ballroom talking, chatting, exchanging favours and information. With the more adventurous nobles dancing in the middle of the ballroom.

Once we were further into the room, Alessandria guided my arm so we started walking clockwise round the room.

Quickly giving my sister a look, I admit she looks good with her long red silk dress. I definitely noticed a few nobles eyeing her up. Yet I think they'll stop once I pass her off to that awful Inquisitor. Which I suspect will find us.

With the band playing smooth jazz in the background, my dull blade spinning in my hand and there being a certain energy in the room, Alessandria whispered to me:

"Are you okay?"

Well, I was looking at a very nice waiter at the time but I don't think that's quite what she meant.

"Yes, I'm fine. I'm using another trick that father taught me,"

"Like what?"

"Well, I'm pretending I'm an assassin and I'm stalking my prey. Meaning I need to remain calm and relaxed not to draw attention to myself,"

"Waiter, another drink please. It's going to be a long night," Alessandria said as she grabbed another glass of champagne.

I jabbed her in the ribs.

"Where's your Inquisitor?"

"I saw him earlier. He thinks he's being stealthy, but I know he's the man in the black hat ten metres to our left,"

"Impressive,"

"Where's your husband to be?"

"I sadly saw him earlier too. He thinks I haven't seen him as he chats up a girl twenty-one metres to our right,"

"A girl?"

"I tried telling Mother, but he is straight. The Earthers only want the money in our military contracts,"

Alessandria cocked her head and smiled.

"You know Mother's too scheming and clever not to know that,"

"I do agree but I still don't want this,"

As Alessandria finished off her second glass, I heard the distinctive footprints of Nemesio coming up behind us. It was actually nice spending time with Alessandria and talking to her. I needed to try and do this more often.

"If you don't want to marry him, I could help,"

I had to laugh.

"You really think you could convince Mother to forget about her plans of making the Earther's business and presumably their mining empire in our fold?"

"Well, you have a point,"

"Dominus Procurator, Freak," Nemesio 'greeted' us both.

I might hate the man with a passion, but I think from the way Alessandria was staring at him, he must have cleaned up nicely. With his fiery red suit and tight shirt that highlighted his muscles.

"Freak may I take your Sister for a dance?"

I unhooked my arm from Alessandria, and I left them.

I was hardly going to waste my time speaking to that idiot.

Looking around, I started to notice that there were a lot more people around me now. My dull blade started to spin quickly.

I felt an arm wrap around my waist.

Quickly I took a deep breath to stop myself from lashing back and putting Geoff in a headlock.

"You look nice," Geoff whispered in my ear.

I gave him a quick look up and down for the sake of being nice, and he did look good in his expensive black suit. That highlighted his muscular body and fine youthful facial features.

"You look good too, I suppose,"

With his arm still unfortunately around my waist, we started walking. Waving politely to the other members of the nobility as we went.

"Who was the girl?" I coldly asked, if I was going to be stuck with him for the night I might as well talk to him.

"Just a commoner. Someone dreaming of the high life,"

"Um, what did you give her?"

"The password to my private house in the hills,"

"Ha," I wanted to say poor soul but even I know that's a bit out of order.

I mean he's taken me to his house before and it's nice, but nothing special.

Looking around at the waiters, I wished I drank. I could use a drink about now.

"I'm surprised you haven't asked about my brother,"

"I know you're emotionless and twisted, so what would that achieve?"

Rolling my eyes, I decided to change our course and make us walk towards Mother who was sitting pridefully on her elevated golden throne on the far side of the ballroom.

"I would have thought when we were married, you would be more... supportive of my special needs,"

"Do not be stupid, Danny. I am certainly not in this for love. We are both here for the sake's of our parents,"

He had a point, but it didn't stop my looking around for Alessandria.

I couldn't see them.

"Pretending you're gay is a bit extreme isn't it?"

"Not when you consider how much the military and weapon contracts your family deals with are worth,"

"We might be the richest Noble Family, but you have the most political power being the oldest family in Ordericous,"

Again, I looked around for Alessandria. I would happily accept the Inquisitor's help at this point.

"We want it all and if that means marrying someone like you. A double freak then I am happy to pay that price,"

Really a double freak?

Finally, we reached Mother sitting on her golden throne. She gave a false smile towards Geoff. She blew a kiss to me.

She came up and gave me a quick hug. I tensed.

"I heard it all," she whispered.

Returning to her throne, she grabbed one of the many empty bottles of wine and she threw it to the ground.

The music stopped and everyone looked at her.

She stumbled slightly forward to the edge of her golden raised platform and started:

"Mighty friends of the House of Fireheart, thank you all for coming. Tonight was meant to be a celebration of my late son Justin and his fiancée. But tonight is a celebration of my only living son, Daniel, and his fiancée Geoff,"

I hated being spoken about in this fashion as the chamber echoed with the clapping of hundreds. It was deafening and disgraceful.

My dull blade spun as fast I could spin it.

Geoff thankfully let go of my waist and he stepped onto my mother's platform.

"Thank you, Lady Fireheart for the kind words. May I please have the floor?"

I tensed for some reason.

"Of course," Mother slowly said and sat back on her throne. A waiter offered her another bottle, but she refused it.

"I regret you inform you all there will be no wedding. I am hereby calling my fellow nobles to arrest Daniel Fireheart and remove the House of Fireheart. For crimes of sexual harassment amongst others. Where Daniel Fireheart tried to force himself on me before I was of legal age,"

My heart stopped.

The entire crowd gasped.

Mother laughed in shock.

These were all lies!

He's older than me for crying out loud! I'm 19, he's 22!

"Arrest him," Geoff Earther said.

I turned around to see five black armoured procurators with the symbol of the Earthers come out.

Mother summoned the Guards.

Alessandria rushed over and stood firmly in front of me.

"Wait!" Mother screamed.

We turned back to Geoff.

"This is an arrest warrant signed by the Order of the Sacred Fire and the House of the Earthers. All that impede this warrant shall be arrested,"

That Inquisitor did this!

The Procurators got closer.

Alessandria stood firm.

The Procurators whipped out their swords.

I needed to run.

The Procurators whacked Alessandria out of the way.

They went to touch me.

Remain calm.

They stretched out their hands to touch me.

Remain calm.

The hands were about to touch me when Nemesio boomed: "By Order of the Inquisition, you will not touch Daniel Fireheart, he is to remain in my custody,"

"You have no authority here, Nobleman," Geoff replied.

"I am no disgusting Nobleman. I am Inquisitor Nemesio of the Order of the Scared Fire. Do as I command, or I will declare your entire House as Traitors,"

Geoff stepped off the stage.

I couldn't see the Inquisitor, but Alessandria turned to me and whispered "Go,"

Instantly, I broke out into a run. Feeling the eyes of hundreds burn into my back. All judging me for the lies of others.

It was all happening again.

CHAPTER 11

Opening the cold iron door handle and stepping through the immense wooden door, Alessandria walked out onto the balcony on top of one of the highest towers in the castle.

She hated it up here. It wasn't too bad tonight but usually the wind was howling and freezing cold.

Stepping out onto the balcony, Alessandria bravely pressed her weight on the cracked grey stone that sent chills up her body.

Once she knew the floor wasn't going to fall away, Alessandria raised her head. Her senses filling with the smell of cooking meat and vegetables from the nearby kitchen. Yet despite the odd gust of wind, everything was peaceful.

Focusing on her surroundings, Alessandria smiled as she saw Daniel sitting safely on yellow stone railings of the balcony, with his legs dangling over the edge.

Well, Alessandria made a quick gasp as she thought about Daniel falling, or something else.

Despite her best efforts, the Dominicus Procurator part of her couldn't help but think about Geoff's action as something more sinister.

Yet as Alessandria took a few steps closer towards her brother none of that mattered, she was his sister and that came first.

Taking careful, measured steps, Alessandria admired her brother for a moment. She had seen him earlier in the ballroom but she was busy thinking about a potential assassination attempt against her Mother. Something she really, really didn't want. Considering she was heir to the House.

However, it was only in the slight light of a nearby window that Alessandria could actually see how good her brother looked. Considering he usually lived in a leather cloak and trousers. Since the formal black suit and trousers with a tiny shine. Definitely highlighted his wealth and status, but it highlighted his slight muscles too.

Alessandria wanted to go into more detail but she shook the thoughts out of her head. Sometimes, she hated her analytical mind!

Once she was within touching distance of Daniel, she stopped and her stomach wanted to flip. What could she say to him after what happened?

She tried to cast her mind back to when Mother and Justin found Daniel's bloodied body. Thankfully, since they did such poor jobs of supporting him. Alessandria didn't exactly have much competition to being the most supportive person to him.

"Beautiful, isn't it?" Alessandria asked she stared out over Ordericous. The towering spires of the Queen's castle with the immense green forests and little lights from the land's citizens were stunning.

"You know I do not do small talk,"

Alessandria rolled her eyes and came up to Daniel. Leaning on the railings, feeling the cold stone press against her dress.

"Anything you want to talk about?"

Alessandria's heart lifted a little as she saw Daniel allowed a small smile to pass over his face.

"You really don't know anything do you?"

"About three years ago, no. I didn't even know three years ago happened. But please, Daniel as your sister and Dominicus Procurator, tell me,"

"Why does it matter? The Order of the Sacred Fire and the rest of the Noble Houses already believe these new lies,"

"Daniel, it's important,"

After a few moments of hesitation, Daniel nodded and replied: "Geoff's already preluded to most of the lies,"

Alessandria wanted to touch or hug Daniel but judging by the speed his dull blade was spinning. That was a terrible idea.

"Three years ago, I lost everything. My friends, my best friends, my respect, dignity and all those other things you *normal* people worry about,"

Alessandria wished she had a drink. She had a feeling this was going to be a difficult talk.

"3 years ago, I was in my final year at school and someone decided to spread lies about me sexually harassing someone and doing worse to a particular person,"

"Harrison Gearing?"

Daniel tensed and his breathing quickened.

Alessandria tensed herself. Expecting she might have to do something.

After a few moments, Daniel took a few deep breaths. To the relief of Alessandria.

"Go on, I'll protect you,"

"Must I talk about him?"

"My beautiful brother, I wish you didn't. But I fear something related to 3 years ago is happening now. Those two hit men. Harrison's name was in their possession. I need you to go and see him,"

Daniel's face was a mixture of fear and utter delight.

"Please Daniel, tell me everything,"

Daniel nodded with great hesitation.

"3 years ago, someone accused me of doing stuff to Harrison. Leading to the school, Procurators, Nobility and even the Orders to get involved,"

Alessandria led harder on the railings trying to catch her breath. Without hearing the story, she knew her brother had been through a lot.

"What happened next?"

"Whoever was behind the lies pressed the investigation as much as they could. I was forced to drop out of school after being beaten within an inch of my life. No one believed I was innocent. I was locked away by Justin. I was completely alone. In the space of two days, I had lost everything,"

"Then what?" Alessandria said in an authoritative tone by accident.

Daniel looked at her.

"Sorry,"

"It's okay. I know you're just doing your job,"

Without thinking, Alessandria gave Daniel a loving hand. He tensed. She didn't let go.

"Daniel, I am your sister and I love you. I will die before I let anything bad happen to you again,"

Daniel nodded his thanks.

Alessandria had no idea if he knew the meaning of the emotional words.

"What happened next?"

"Well, I was friendless. My family hardly supported me. My future was over for all I cared. So, I grabbed a knife and you saw the results,"

Alessandria squeezed her brother's hands some more.

"I'm sorry Daniel. I really am. But can I be a Dominicus procurator?"

He nodded.

"How did Geoff know? What happened to the investigation?"

Daniel smiled a little.

"I have no idea how Geoff knew. The entire event 3 years ago was strange. Before I lost my mind briefly, I suspected the liar was something in the Noble Houses,"

"Makes sense. Explains how the Earthers knew about it. What about the investigation?"

"I don't know. I wasn't told anything. All I was told by a very angry and judgemental Justin was I was to remain in the castle. Then a few days later I was shipped off to do military service for two years,"

"Wait, two years? You came back after 3 months. Was it your autism?"

"Ha, no. And I prefer you don't ask why I was exiled,"

"Fine enough, what did Mother do?"

"Mother was pleased to have me back. She forced me to spend the night I returned with her,"

"And Justin?"

"He actually beat me,"

Alessandria's stomach flipped.

"He beat me, and he actually tried to finish what I tried three years ago,"

CHAPTER 12

Never in a million years would I have imagined I would have told Alessandria about three years ago like that. I always imagined I'll tell her in a more relaxed way.

I still hate Justin with a passion. How could he hate me so much that he would want to kill me?

Anyway, Alessandria gave me Harrison's address and a horse, the smelly thing, and I'm approaching his house now.

Looking around and seeing the rolling hills with the olive trees and dry sandy yellow road with fields surrounding the area. I definitely think this is a nice place.

No doubt Mother would have killed to get a place like this in the hills, further away from the city. And most importantly close to the Queen's vineyards.

Turning my head from side to side, I admired the waist high stone walls that lined the sandy road with the large rough olive woods blowing slightly in the night wind.

Although, I didn't like the creepiness of the area. I was a lone man walking along a dirt road in the middle of nowhere. Without a mouse or cricket stirring and the full moon shining bright. Sounds like the beginning of a horror novel!

Regardless, I tried to banish the thoughts from my head and I kept walking. Feeling the rough cracked ground press into my feet. Trying to break my ankles.

Looking down the road, I saw the little rectangular house with its single store and thick thatch roof. It looked nice. I'm not sure if I liked the white and blue paint. Yet I certainly liked the small garden with some vegetables around the place.

Personally, I did enjoy a bit of gardening. Before father gave me my dull blade. Hacking away dead plants was another source of stress relief.

As I got closer to the little house, I could smell the, I suppose, pleasant smells of cooked meats and sweet flowers. I didn't know if they were that pleasant, I just know other people think so.

Then I had to stop when I was almost in front of the house.

Staring at the grey stoned path, with burning candles that smelt disgusting on either side, leading to the wooden door. I knew I really didn't want to do this.

I was about to see the only man I've ever loved for the first time in three years. What if he doesn't want to see me?

What if people lied to him saying I was guilty of something?

What if I had changed and he hated me?

Or what if he changed into something I hated?

Looking down at my hand, I hadn't realised how fast my dull blade was spinning. So, I forced myself to take a few deep breaths. And anyway, at the end of the day, I was here as a representative of the House of Fireheart. Looking into the thankful... I mean devastating murder of Justin. But I still love to get my friend back.

A part of me still wanted to find out the truth about three years ago but from my military services, I know the truth can sometimes be just as painful. And I really don't want to be in the same mental state as three years ago.

I gently rubbed my arms.

Two years ago I promised myself I would never be like that again, but everything already felt as if it was against me.

Forcing myself to take steps towards the door, my heart was starting to pound.

The door opened.

My heart skipped a few beats.

Harrison popped out.

"Daniel, what are you doing here? Are you trying to get me killed?"

CHAPTER 13

Wiping the tears from her eyes in the dark stairwell, Alessandria forced herself to relax and stop being her brother's sister. For now, her family needed her to be the Dominicus Procurator she was born to be. Her family needed her to find the truth. So, brushing her tears away, Alessandria straightened her back and walked out into the corridor where Nemesio was keeping Geoff contained.

However, she almost gagged at the strange rotten egg smell that filled her nose. She looked at the stone floor quickly and saw someone had dropped some furry sandwiches on the floor. She rolled her eyes and made a mental note to get a maid to come here later. For now, she had bigger problems.

The two men in the far distance didn't see or hear her coming, so Alessandria decided to approach them gracefully and slowly. This was probably for the best. Best not to let Geoff know of the damage he had done.

As she stalked the cold stone corridor with metre thick stone blocks either side her, Alessandria had to snarl at the disgraceful Geoff. He was not noble, he never had been.

A part of her hated herself for not showing enough interest or care to check if he was right for the family.

Another part of her hated Kinaaz for being so scheming. Ignoring the clear threat the Earthers posed. And her mother had to know he was straight, so why put Daniel through that?

Alessandria looked down at her hands to see she had formed fists without realising it. She took a deep breath and remembered a bizarre conversation she had once had with Kinaaz. It was something about she knew everything about her noble counterparts and that kept them safe.

The Dominicus Procurator had no idea what that truly meant but that's another reason why she never wanted to be Lady Fireheart. She didn't want to be constantly looking out for assassins.

Attempting to shake away the bad thoughts, including her hate towards Justin, Alessandria's eyes narrowed on Geoff as she got closer.

Nemesio in his fiery armour turned around and gave Alessandria a false smile. He probably wanted to know what so-called evidence she was destroying.

When Alessandria stopped, her feet made a loud bang on the cold hard stone floor. She stared with hate at the boldness of Geoff. She wanted him to pay.

Unfortunately, Geoff opened his mouth first.

"Oh Alessandria, I was telling your Inquisitor about the crazy stick holding woman by the door. I think she's going to attack the party. I had to run away from her,"

Alessandria had to give her friend credit when it was due. Hellen definitely knew how to prevent people from escaping.

"Ha, dearest traitorous Earther. What were you playing at tonight?"

Geoff gave a devilish smile at the other two.

"Alessandria Fireheart, you cannot touch me. Your Inquisitor will not let you,"

The Dominicus Procurator's eyes narrowed on Nemesio.

Through controlled rage, she managed: "What is he talking about?"

"Relax now Noble scum, he has committed no crimes tonight. Yet he has told me plenty of your family's crimes against the Crown,"

"What!"

"Yes, there are plenty. I will be investigating them all,"

"We are being set up!"

"If that is true then my Inquisitorial investigation will prove it,"

Alessandria was too confused for words.

"Now, Lady Fireheart, I must leave. I have ordered your guests to be released and none are to be charged. I must report to the Order,"

Alessandria's mouth dropped as the Inquisitor stormed off.

Geoff grinned at her.

"See, I am untouchable. Unlike your freak of

a brother,"

"My brother might be different but he smarter than all of us combined,"

"Ha. Since you cannot touch me, Fireheart. I will tell you this. The country is changing. The Queen will fall and sides must be picked. Make sure you liberals are ready to die,"

"You forget Earther scum, you are a gay abomination in the eyes of the people. You too will die if the laws are changed,"

"Not if I tell the people, your brother forced me to be gay at the threat of mine's and my family's lives. You hold no power here Fireheart,"

Geoff started to walk away.

"Why? What was the point of all of this?" she called out.

"Old wounds have resurfaced tonight. The entire nobility knows about three years ago now. Everyone knows Daniel Fireheart and your House are criminals. The Orders will find him guilty this time,"

"Did you start the lies?"

"You cannot arrest me,"

"I don't care. Who started the lies?"

Geoff walked off. His feet tapping against the cold hard stone. Before he shouted: "Ask your mother?"

Before Alessandria could go after him, she smelt the fruity scents of aged wine and her mother tapped her on the shoulder.

"What did that pig want?"

"You're sober?" she laughed.

Kinaaz just looked at her.

"Sorry, I'll say that with a straight face. You're… no sorry I can't,"

"Yes, I am sober. I've not had a drink for an hour. Thank you,"

Alessandria jokingly fell onto a wall.

Her mother kicked her.

"What did the pig want?"

"He glowed that we cannot touch him, or his family and our House will fall,"

"I admit this changes the scheme,"

"The scheme?"

"Ah, yes. Um. Well, this was sort of planned but this has got a bit out of hand now,"

"Mother, what did you do?"

"Well, I may have implicitly implied the Earthers should kill… Annalise. Then I could remove them for the murder,"

"Oh, Mother!"

"What it's a benefit that Justin died,"

"What!"

"Do not play games with me, Alexis. I know Daniel told you about three years ago,"

"Yea, Justin was hardly a good brother and son!"

"What do you mean? He was practically your pet?"

Kinaaz stared with rage then sorrow in her eyes.

She rolled up her sleeves to reveal large black bruises.

"Your brother was foul. I protected you so much,"

CHAPTER 14

After firmly telling Harrison that Justin was dead, he reluctantly allowed me inside. But only after he did a quick check of the perimeter. This is ridiculous! Why do I think I'm about to discover another disgusting thing about Justin?

Anyway, as I stepped through the door, I kept walking into the living room. I heard the wooden door shut behind me and the click of the lock. I didn't care.

For the first time in three years, all tension from my body was gone and my dull blade didn't spin. I just loosely held it.

I had to admit Harrison's place, he had done well for himself or someone had given him the house. The hot air from the Roaring fire in the far right hand corner made the room warm and pleasant. Unlike outside!

I bet it looked as if I was inspecting the place. (I was but I wanted to be discreet) Regardless of that I looked at the beautiful roaring fire with the large brown fur rug in front next to a well sized coffee table.

Yet my favourite feature about the living room was the two expensive grey fabric sofas around the coffee table. I knew he hadn't bought them, far too expensive for... a commoner.

I wanted to turn around and face Harrison but I was too scared. I still didn't want to open this can of worms. The last time we spoke we were best friends then everything happened with the lies and... I don't know.

Slowly, I made myself turn around, seeing the wooden walls of cabinets attached, to face Harrison.

He gave me a friendly smile. Neither one of us wanted to be the first person to talk. Then I realised a very pleasant fact. He was topless.

I must have smiled without knowing as he gave a little chuckle.

I didn't care in the slightest as I looked at his smooth thin waist and well defined six pack. His smooth chest and wonderful biceps.

In all honesty, he was the definition of beautiful with his muscles and youthful face with his strong jaw line. But if he was clothed, which I really didn't want, you wouldn't be able to tell he had muscles. Sure, you could tell he was thin but not muscular.

As I looked at him, I thought about all of the rubbish and ridiculousness I have had to deal with over the past three years. And I just thought how much I wanted to relax.

Without thinking, I just walked over to Harrison and hugged him tight. I needed my friend. Whatever fantasies I ever had about Harrison, he was always my friend first and that's what I needed.

In his smooth beautiful voice, Harrison asked:

"So Justin's dead. How are you doing?"

Well, that was a mood killer as a strange warmth engulfed my arms. I pushed away and walked over to his three piece sofa. As I sat down the warm soft material moulded to my body. He definitely didn't buy this.

"You know how it is. I rarely feel things for other people,"

"Except me,"

"Well,"

How could I reply to that?

"How have you been Daniel?"

"My dearest Harrison, we are both autistic. We do not need to act like the people who bullied us at school,"

"Good point, why are you here?"

"Your name came up in the investigation into Justin's fortunate death,"

Harrison walked over to the sofa and sat on the other end, smiling at me.

"Your sister's actually investigation. Does she know he did to us? Your mother?"

Now, he had my attention.

"How did you know about Mother? Alessandria doesn't even know,"

Harrison placed his hands over his face for a moment.

"I forget you don't know what happened to me. But I guess I don't know what happened to you either,"

A part of me so badly wanted to know but my arms were burning up. I needed to take off my shirt but that felt a little inappropriate.

"Did two hitmen come and see you recently?"

"What the Domo Brothers?"

"I think that's what Alessandria called them when she showed me the file,"

"Yea, they came… three days ago. They wanted to know about carriages and the House of Fireheart,"

I frowned.

"I refused to talk about your House but the carriages I explained the basics,"

"Carriages?"

"Yea, I'm the Queen's Chief Engineer. Surely Justin…"

Despite me wanting to never know what happened I had to know. I had to know what Justin did to the only person I've ever truly cared about.

"Please tell me everything, Harrison,"

He paused. He gave a caring smile and he began:

"I was in class one day. The Headteacher and Representatives of the Order came in and the Order Inquisitor told me what I say if I was questioned. They ordered me to confirm the story that you did something to me. Or they would kill my brother and father and erase them from history,"

"But you were never questioned,"

"No then the Inquisitor handed me over to

Justin and he explained to me with a knife at my throat. I was never to see you again or contact you or your House. He got me the job as Chief Engineer and he got me this land as payment,"

I was still silent.

"Daniel, I refused at first. Justin left and my father was found dead a few hours later. They said he was burned alive after someone had pumped his stomach full of alcohol and lit it,"

"That's a shame. There, there,"

Harrison had a loud laugh at my inability to be comforting.

"Wait what about your friends and everything?" I asked.

"Daniel, I wasn't allowed back. That day I lost all my friends, my girlfriend, and my future. I never got my education unlike you,"

I cocked my head.

"What do you mean, unlike me? I was trapped in my room then shipped off to war. I was meant to die. I wanted to go to university, get a good job and live my life. I never wanted this,"

Harrison's head dropped. Clearly, feeling bad for his comments.

"Our lives never were easy, were they? From the people bullying you to the people never wanting us to be friends to well everything in between," I explained.

He opened his arms to me.

"Like the old times,"

Knowing what he meant, I climbed over to the other side of the sofa and I cuddled him. He wrapped his arms around me.

There was nothing remotely sexual about this. I smiled as I remembered us doing this in the past. Unlike, Harrison I couldn't afford to lash out when the world was too much, so I needed contact. As I rested the back of my head on his chest, I barely heard his beating heart.

"You aren't wrong. We didn't have the easiest of friendships. No one would allow us any time to ourselves," he added.

"Only because no one understood I needed time only. I hate people and large groups. No one ever asked why I did what I did. No one even tried to understand me. Everyone thought I was a freak and didn't try to understand,"

"They didn't know you were autistic. They didn't know you needed help,"

"You did. Thank you,"

"You're welcome. Why are you here at 11 o'clock at night? I just got in from work and I was about to take a bath,"

My eyes widened at the image.

"Really?"

He hit me on the head.

"Wait, you still love me,"

"Of course,"

"Why are you here so late in a suit?"

Change the subject why don't you? I wanted

to say but I behaved myself. Alessandria would be proud.

"The Earthers exposed three years ago and everyone in the country thinks I did something to Geoff Earther and you,"

"The Earthers?"

"Yes, you know something,"

"Lord Earther came to see me on the day of the murder. He wanted to know about Justin and the weaknesses of your House. He offered me a lot of coin and his son, but I refused,"

"Strange, the Earthers are up to something. I need to go and tell Alessandria," I tapped Harrison's arm and he let go. Walking towards the door, I said: "It's great seeing you again,"

"Daniel, will you come back?"

"Yea maybe… wait Lord Earther offered you his son? Why would he do that?"

A slightly boyish grin appeared on Harrison's face.

"Well, Daniel I'm not exactly into girls anymore,"

Wow. Was I meant to be pleased? Excited? I couldn't deal with that idea right now.

"I need to talk to Alessandria,"

Touching the cold door handle to leave I was about to leave when Harrison said: "Daniel, it's late at night. The criminals will be on the streets now. Please stay. Stay with me,"

CHAPTER 15

With a heavy head and the stupidly hot beaming sun on her, Alessandria dragged herself along the yellow sandy dirt road, with the rolling hills around her, as she walked towards Harrison's house. A part of Alessandria was more than proud of her brother for staying the night with him. Then the other part, the Procurator part, really wished he hadn't. If it got out, it would make her job harder.

Yet Alessandria or the alcohol shook the thoughts away. The Dominicus Procurator still couldn't believe how much she drank last night when she got to her bedroom and firmly locked the door. She hated herself for feeling the need to drown her problems in six bottles of wine. But she wasn't going to be hard on herself. Not after learning how awful Justin was. How could someone abuse their own mother?

Alessandria kissed her mother on the head last night after they both had a heart to heart in her mother's Chambers. She still didn't want to believe it. Her brother, her strong brother, the person she admired and loved, tried to kill her brother and abused her mother as soon as father died.

Shaking her head, Alessandria could partially understand his anger at father's death but this was all extreme.

Tears started to swell up in her eyes.

Especially, at the memory of Kinaaz telling her most of her beatings were from her telling Justin Alessandria was off limits.

Again, her mother continued to surprise her with her love. But it explained her drinking. After last night, she could relate.

Trying to forget about the past, she tried to focus on the present and making sure her House survived, and hopefully recover from Justin's tyranny.

Taking a deep breath, Alessandria allowed the beautiful scent of the nearby wild flowers and grapes from the vineyards to fill her nose. They smelt great. No wonder Harrison hadn't moved.

Then she remembered Justin's personal file Hellen had found. What Justin did and forced Harrison to do was monstrous. She needed to fix everything. She was the Dominicus Procurator now. Surely, Alessandria could right all the wrongs Justin did?

Walking up to the door, Alessandria hesitated. She really didn't want to interrupt her brother, but she needed to know about Harrison.

She knocked on the door.

"Daniel, I know you're in there. I need to talk to you,"

Something smashed on the floor and sounds of fast movements came from inside. Then the door opened, and Daniel came back. Tucking his shirt into his trousers.

"Good night?"

Daniel smiled. The first time in a long time.

"It wasn't like that, but it was nice,"

Daniel started to walk away so Alessandria followed.

"How is he?"

"Considering what happened. He did a lot better than me,"

Alessandria went to hug him, but he backed away quickly.

"Please don't,"

She gave him a nod of respect.

"So what happened last night between you two,"

"I think I should ask you that. You're clearly struggling to walk in a straight line and your breath stinks,"

"Direct as always,"

"I am here for you too, Alessandria,"

Her head became a bit clearer at the words, but she still didn't know how to talk to Daniel about her own rage towards Justin. And that's before she considered the guilt, she carried over not knowing, let alone not being able to protect her Mother and Daniel.

"One day, we will talk properly about both our pain towards him. But we need to save our House first,"

Daniel nodded.

"Did you get what we needed?"

"Yes, it's the Earthers. The Lord Earther in particular seems too interested in us, our weaknesses and Justin,"

Alessandria nodded.

Daniel kept smiling.

"You found out about Harrison's preference, didn't you?"

"How did you know?"

Alessandria rolled her eyes and smiled as she walked into that question.

"Justin sort of kept a file on him. Hellen found it. Do you want to read it?"

"Burn it,"

"Of course,"

Daniel's eyes widened as he realised that was a bit rude.

"Sorry, no thank you. But it was nice finding out,"

"So what happened last night?"

"Nothing. We just stayed up and cached up. You know he's one of three people in the Kingdom that doesn't need an appointment to see the Queen. Then we slept together,"

Just because Alessandria knew Hellen would ask later: "Clothed?"

Daniel shook his head at Alessandria's question: "Yes, our lower half at least,"

Tens of heavy footfalls of horses filled the

road.

Alessandria spun around.

She saw six fiery red horses storm towards them.

Their hooves were deafening.

Her and Daniel started to run.

Two horses flew past them.

The riders were wearing black masks and fiery red and blue armour.

Alessandria bit her lips in annoyance.

The horses turned around and charged towards them.

Alessandria dived to one side.

She tried to get up.

Another two horses charged over to her.

She rolled over and over.

Trying to dodge the hooves.

One rider jumped off their horse. Running over to her.

She jumped up.

The rider wearing the symbol of the Inquisition threw sand in her eyes and kicked her to the ground.

Alessandria rubbed her eyes as she heard the horses ride away.

Looking around Alessandria screamed in horror as she realised Daniel was gone. His dulled blade laying there in the road.

CHAPTER 16

Flicking Daniel's dull blade in her hands, Alessandria understood why her brother had found playing with this so relaxing. Yet her mind was still spinning.

In truth, Alessandria looked around with hate at all her folders and files sitting in the bookshelves on the walls. Even her immense brown oak desk looked futile, she so badly wanted to smash it up. How could the Inquisition take Daniel?

She had sent Procurator after Procurator to their temple and they all came back saying they were stopping tens of metres before the door.

What the most irritating thing about her brother being taken was Nemeiso had abandoned her. He didn't even have the decency to explain his actions to her. He had to be behind it.

Nemesio, the so-called noble Inquisitor must have ordered the Inquisition's chamber militants to take Daniel.

Then Alessandria had to laugh at how stupid Nemeiso was believing Geoff Earther. All of them were going to pay.

Taking a deep breath to calm herself, Alessandria focused on the present. Allowing her body to feel the hardness of the wooden chair she sat on and she breathed in the smell of old books and paper from her bookshelves.

Looking at the clock on her desk, she tutted and raised her head to see if Hellen was around.

After Daniel had been taken, she ordered a female servant to go and get her. Alessandria had learnt the hard way not to sent male servants to see Hellen. She loved her best friend but she did worry about her. She deserved to be loved and appreciated by proper men, not quickies in the night.

Shaking her head clear of those interesting images, Alessandria thought hard about the Inquisition. They had gone way too far this time. Investigating her House, taking her brother and probably torturing him. Enough was enough.

A tear swelled up in her eye as she remembered the horrific tales of whipping, slashing and beatings from people who barely survived the Inquisition.

Although that wasn't Alessandria's true concern as she played with Daniel's dull blade. Daniel had weaknesses, other people do not. The Interrogators would use them against him. She had to find him.

In that moment, she did not care one bit about the consequences but she would get the Inquisition abolished. If not for Daniel then for the tens of thousands that were tortured or perished since their creation over a millennium ago.

At last, Alessandria heard the typical tapping of wood hitting a stone floor as Hellen walked in.

Wearing her grey Procurator coat but her boots and black armour were coated in thick mud. At least judging by the smell Alessandria really hoped it was all mud and not a mixture of something else.

"I'm sorry about your brother. How ya doing?"

"In the past few days, I've found out my brother was abusive and a monster. How do you think I feel!"

Hellen's eyes widened at Alessandria's tone.

"I... I'm sorry. It's been a hard few days,"

"It's okay. Ya know what I like to do when I'm stressed,"

Resting her smiling face in her hands, Alessandria answered: "Everyone knows what you do whether you're stressed or not. But no I don't need any *stress relief*. Thank you,"

"That's a shame. I could have fixed ya up with a perfect man,"

"What did your Dominicus Procurator say?"

"Ah, officially it is not in the interest of the Majestic Procurators to pick a fight with the Orders,"

"And Unofficially?"

"She's sorry about Daniel but she doesn't have the political power or influence to do anything. But she did manage to confirm Daniel is being held at their temple,"

"Wait, she can firm his whereabouts but not do anything?"

"Ya, we watch the Orders carefully. We know

a lot more about them than they would like us to know,"

"Really, what's happening to Daniel?"

"Again, officially, he's only being questioned. But we both know the reality,"

Alessandria slammed her fists into the desk.

"I will get him back!"

"We always get ya bad guys,"

"Not this time, I have a very important job for you,"

Hellen leaned in closer.

"You know the Warlock that saved Daniel after his… incident?"

"Ya, some outlawed warlock. I'm surprised the Inquisition hasn't tried to get ya done for that. Why not use a healer?"

"For starters, the wounds were too severe for herbals and medicine. And healers can't heal self-inflicted wounds. Hence, the need for a warlock or witch,"

"Where is he? Wait, why ya need me?"

"Because you're the only person I trust to do this for me. I need you to travel to Helixo Bay in the far North. He will find you. Say I sent you. I need you to get a sanity potion for me,"

"Of course. I'll leave now,"

Hellen got up.

Alessandria walked around the desk and hugged her friend.

"Safe travels and be quick. People will be

hunting you. And the warlock is a woman in case you were getting ideas,"

Hellen rolled her eyes and ran out the room.

Alessandria walked back over to her desk. Allowing the hard wood to chill her bones again. Then Nemesio walked in.

His blue and red fiery armour a disgrace.

His sweaty smell an assault on the senses.

Alessandria grabbed the clock and threw it at him.

Nemesio grunted with pain.

Alexis jumped up and ran at him.

He was a dirty Inquisitor. The man responsible for Daniel's kidnapping. He would pay.

She grabbed him by the throat.

Throwing his head into the desk.

Her hand was covered in his blood.

Alessandria flipped over and pinned him to the desk.

"Why! What did Daniel do!"

"I am sorry,"

Alessandria whacked him across the face.

"That's not good enough. Declare me traitor or whatever. I will kill you,"

"You were set up. I am sorry. I am stupid. I should have seen it earlier. Please kill me,"

Alessandria cocked her head.

"Tell me everything!"

"My Order is not innocent. My Order planned it all,"

The Dominicus Procurator released him.

"Speak,"

"The Earthers and the Order of the Sacred Fire teamed up and conspired to take down your House. You're too liberal for them. The Queen is too liberal as well. With you gone, the Queen is weakened. Then my former Order could raise,"

"Your former Order?"

"Lady Fireheart, I promise you I am not homophobic. I might have my problems with the nobility. But I have no problems with the House of Fireheart,"

"Liar,"

"No, I promise. You don't know what it's like to be an Inquisitor for an extreme Order. I had to become an Inquisitor to survive. They kill and beat their servants for fun,"

"Why not leave!"

"The Order was everything to me after the Nobility killed my village,"

Alessandria shook her head. She wasn't going to be sympathetic.

"Why take Daniel?"

"Because he is the definition of an abomination. His autism makes him a pollutant on the human gene pool in their eyes. His homosexuality makes him a freak and an offensive against their teachings,"

"I will kill them all,"

"I have no doubt, Lady Fireheart. Please let

me help you. I must earn penance,"

"You, help me! This is your fault,"

Alessandria had to do everything in her power not to kill him.

"Release my brother and I will consider your help,"

"I cannot release him. The Mage of the Order demanded Daniel's imprisonment. Only the Mage or… I don't think there is someone higher can get him released,"

"Where is your Mage!"

"Ha! I like your spirit Alessandria. But even you will not be able to get to her in the Temple. You would need an army. A proper one, not your House squads,"

"Would a confession from the Earthers help?"

"I doubt it but a confession might help unite the other Orders against the Mage. In the Inquisition, in theory anyone can order a conclave. If the three other Mages vote in our favour, it can force the Scared Fire Mage to release Daniel,"

Alessandria shot up and stormed out the door.

Nemesio sat there.

"Are you coming Inquisitor!"

CHAPTER 17

Stepping into the meeting chamber of the Earthers, Alessandria looked around with hate and disdain. You could easily tell this was a mining family with the entire massive chamber being made from solid polished steel. Along with grand ugly pillars of green copper running down the sides of the chamber.

With all the money the Earthers had it was surprising they didn't have nicer things.

Even though, Alessandria's eyes widened as she tried to work out what was good about having a polished bronze floor. If anything, the weird reflection made her look very large.

The strange thing about the chamber was the odd smell of metallic and nothing else. Even your mouth was full of a metallic taste.

Looking forward, Alessandria shook her head at the walls as they were covered in so-called pieces of metal art. She wondered how much the Earthers were paying the toddler who made these ugly creations.

The Inquisitor walked past her, his feet banging against the polished bronze. She gave him a little snarl. Alessandria still wanted to kill him. If he didn't report his 'important' evidence to his Mage then maybe she could have prevented this.

Maybe she could save her brother's mind. The stories from survivors were never good.

Casting her mind back to a few months ago, she remembered a young boy probably Daniel's age and he had tried to burn himself alive. She stopped him but he screamed at her. Telling her about the nightmares and memories of the rats, beatings and magically induced horrors. Yet what most alarmed Alessandria was the story about the Witch that could make you relive the worse part of your life, and make it feel worse.

Now, that wouldn't worry Alessandria if it was another person. But considering Daniel tried to end it all in the most painful way possible, she knew she needed to hurry up and save him.

She looked around for the Earthers but they weren't here. Alessandria hoped they would meet them. It was only because of Nemesio's authority they got in the door.

After a few more seconds, Alessandria heard heavy footsteps behind them. the Dominicus Procurator turned around and she grinned as she saw Lord Earther walking towards her.

His heavy built clear evidence of enjoying the Noble lifestyle too much and his thick brown fur coat covered up his even thicker armour.

Alessandria met his cold green eyes, yet she was repulsed by his angelic well-aged face.

The closer the Lord got to her, the more Alessandria could smell fat and rich meats. That wasn't pleasant.

"Welcome, welcome, welcome Alessandria. If you told me you were coming. I would have let you in. No need for your... man to demand entry,"

"Do not play games, *Lord*. You are involved in crimes against the House of Fireheart. I do as I please,"

"Ha. Clearly you do not. Did you want your freak of a brother taken?"

Alessandria's eyes narrowed.

"Repent,"

"I have nothing to Repent. I am innocent,"

"You are a liar. I have evidence,"

"No, little Fireheart. So much fire, so little brain,"

"You will repent or I will arrest you,"

"You cannot do that. My Dominicus has more friends than you do. He will see to it that I am released, and you arrested for Abuse of Power,"

"I will give my evidence to the Queen and she will decide your fate,"

"Ha! That stupid woman. Her reign is almost over after ten months. She means nothing. What is this great evidence? That freak Harrison Gearing. It's easy to argue, he's mentally unfit. And as for your Inquisitor. Well, where do I begin? His Order hates him for saving heretics and abominations. They will not believe him,"

Nemesio's hands formed fists.

"No Inquisitor," Alessandria snarled.

"Anyway, little Fireheart I will make this easier for you,"

Alessandria gave him a small smile.

"You cannot touch me that is simple. Yes, I ordered the death of your brother. Yes, I am working with the Order to take you down in exchange for becoming King. Yes, I ordered Geoff to reveal your brother's pathetic life to the masses,"

Alessandria wanted to kill him, rip him apart and feed him to the wolves. But she stopped herself.

"You are weak and stupid. You really think the Order will give you independence. You will be their puppet,"

"Not unless I abolish them,"

"That will not work. They will simply work in the shadows,"

"Maybe but let's see,"

Lord Earther walked away and shouted: "You better hurry little Fireheart. The average prisoner lasts twenty-four hours. Tick tock,"

Alessandria spat on his polished floor and smeared the mud on her boots over the floor.

Nemesio smiled, shook his head and did the same.

The Dominicus Procurator started to walk away.

"What now?" Nemesio asked.

"We go to the one person who can overrule the Inquisition,"

CHAPTER 18

With the sun burning bright orange over the churning dark blue sea, Alessandria stared over the harbour as she waited for Inquisitor Nemesio to join her.

Looking across the harbour, Alessandria smiled as she remembered coming here often as a child. Helping the maids buy fresh fish from the crowded market stalls on the far side of the harbour. Next to the large red, blue and white buildings that surrounded the harbour.

She wished whoever was in charge of the harbour would deal with the gangs and drug smugglers calling these buildings home. But unless these gangs or drugs were found on her land, she had no power.

Rolling her eyes at the futile fact, she was powerless everywhere except her own land. Alessandria focused on the breathing view of the harbour with the immense sea wall, home to Archers and the Royal Navy gunners, that sheltered a stunning range of boats. From the little colourful fishing boats of the commoners to the posh well crafted wooden ships of the nobility to the mighty fleets of the Queen in the distance.

The salty wind of the sea started to blow strong against the harbour. Her hair blew wildly and the ships clanged and banged as they rocked.

It didn't take Alessandria long to want some water to get rid of the thick salty taste in her mouth and to wash away the salt crystals on her skin. Where was Nemesio?

A part of her wondered if he was betraying her family again but he seemed horrified around Daniel's kidnapping. Still, Alessandria wanted to beat him and punish him. Maybe she could push him into the water. She shook the dark thoughts away, tempting as they'll be.

With the wind intensifying and more salt starting to cover her black cloak, Alessandria turned around to face the immense thousand year old lighthouse. Considering it was ancient, even Alessandria could appreciate it. With its massive blocks of solid black granite and it raising into the sky for over a kilometre.

Looking at the much newer wooden door. Alessandria grabbed the freezing salt encrusted door ring and pulled.

It didn't open.

Looking over her shoulder, she saw the harbour was clear and she smashed the door open.

Immediately, Alessandria coughed as a foul mustardy smell came through the lighthouse, but walked inside.

Despite the darkness, Alessandria could still make out the rough granite walls and the cruelly made circling granite staircase that went to the top.

She couldn't even begin to understand what it was like for the ancient workers having to travel up a dangerous staircase every day.

Turning around the sound of heavy footsteps on the granite floor, Alessandria saw Nemesio sneered at the lighthouse as he entered.

Without saying a word, Alessandria started to walk up the thousands of steps towards the top. Feeling the sharp shards of the granite press against her leather boots and the stale air of the Lighthouse greeting her lungs. Nemesio quickly followed.

"Why did you call me here?"

Alessandria smiled.

"I demand to know. I was checking out the Order's Temple. Security has increased,"

"That is why we are here Inquisitor,"

"What? At a lighthouse no one has used or step foot in for over nine hundred years,"

"Back in the day, this Lighthouse was vital to Ordericous' security,"

"How do you know that? Only the most senior Inquisitors have access to such records,"

"Ha, Daniel has many ways to acquire information. He refers to it as the only permeant currency,"

"I knew he was dirty!"

"Inquisitor, you are hardly convincing me not to kill you,"

"Oh, sorry. Old habits…"

"I do not care. Break them or I break you,"

Alessandria heard Nemesio paused for a second before continuing.

"So, why are we here?"

"Because we need to talk to the only person who can overrule the Inquisition,"

"And I will repeat myself, there is no one,"

"Incorrect, the Inquisition answers to the Throne,"

"Oh, that's an ancient rule that no one listens to,"

"As Daniel informs me, no one has listened to the law since the murder of King Alfredic over six centuries ago. Yet the law is still written and must be listened to,"

"The Queen will not listen,"

"She will,"

"I am sorry. She is weak. A toy to the nobility and influencers,"

"She is honest,"

"She has no power. No friends,"

"I am her friend,"

"Your House means nothing,"

"We have the coin to change minds,"

Nemesio went silent.

"Anyway what's your plan? Why not go to the Queen?"

"Ha! I cannot simply go to see the Queen. The Guards will not allow me in or anyone from my House,"

"So, your plan has failed,"

"Negative. Me and the Queen served together overseas when her father lived. After one too many drinks, she revealed there's an ancient protocol that states if the lighthouse is lit. The Queen must come,"

"A bit of a long shot,"

"At least I am doing something to save my brother. What are you doing? You got him in this mess,"

Nemesio once again went silent.

Alessandria continued to walk up the constant stream of circling steps. The air was old and stale. Alessandria smelt her leather from time to time to clear her senses.

"I am sorry. I reached out to the other Inquisitors in the other Orders. They will not help. They prefer to stay clear of the Sacred Fire, but they wouldn't take revenge on you if that Order disappeared,"

"How typical of you lot. All talk and no action,"

Alessandria smiled in the darkness as she noted they were a third of the way up the Lighthouse. Her head slightly dizzy from going round and round.

Turning her head slightly, she barely managed to see Nemesio frowning with something like a tear in his eye at her hateful words.

"What will you do when the Queen shows up?"

"I'll get her to order Daniel's release,"

"If she doesn't,"

"I will do whatever she wants to secure Daniel's release,"

"What if nothing is worth the fallout of his release?"

"Then I'll have to kidnap her,"

CONNOR WHITELEY

CHAPTER 19

After an extremely dizzy walk and listening to a very annoying Inquisitor, Alessandria finally made it to the top of the Lighthouse and lit the brazier. That was hours ago.

With heavy eyelids, Alessandria watched as the once beautiful stack of wood in its dirty gold dish went out as the last few embers died.

For the past eight hours, her and Nemesio had sat here waiting for her old friend to come. But the Queen must have abandoned them.

The emotional part of Alessandria wanted to cry and scream her rage into the salty wind of the harbour. But her Procurator side knew the Queen couldn't just walk out to meet her. The number of Guards that would have to 'fall asleep' so she could escape was ridiculous.

Alessandria rolled over. The freezing cold black granite chilling her to the bone. At least her legs still felt the warmth of the gold dish and the leftover heat from the fire.

When she turned over, she rested her head on some carved out granite in the shape of a seat and looked out over the harbour. Seeing the little boats in the harbour and the mightiest navy ships patrolling the waters.

Joyous memories of love and family time played across her mind as she remembered the chaotic days she had when her father had thought it a great idea to take a boat out.

Daniel hated it. The loud wind, the choppy water and he got whacked in the back of the head with that bottom part of the sail. The *boom* Alessandria remembered.

Those were the days when everything was fun and they were a true family. She missed those days. Maybe when Daniel was free, she'll take him and Mother out. Maybe.

She closed her eyes. Listening to the great all powerful wind whipping across the Lighthouse. At least at this height you weren't coated in a layer of salt crystals.

Then doubt started to fill her mind. What was she really doing here?

She could have raided the temple by now and probably died. But Alessandria would rather be dying or fighting than just sitting here thinking about what Daniel was going through.

Rolling over again, Alessandria opened her eyes and stared at the sleeping Inquisitor in his tight fiery red and blue armour. She hated her tired mind because it would do things her rational self would never do. Like admit how attractive Nemesio was with his masculine features and muscles.

However, there was something about him too she liked. Maybe it was his duty to the truth, as misguided as it was, or something else but there was more to Nemesio than the almighty Inquisitor act.

He opened his eyes and smiled at her.

"Didn't she show?"

"No, Inquisitor. We've just wasted eight hours. Daniel could be dead by now,"

"Unlikely. The... sessions can go for days or weeks,"

"Not helping,"

Nemesio stood up and walked over to sit next to Alessandria. Again her tired mind played the game of leaning into him. Alessandria could feel his body warmth and muscles.

"Why do you hate me so much, Nemesio?"

"Ha. You're probably the only House I remotely like. I was a peasant once. Me and my mother farmed the land for a Noble House when I was five years old. My father and brothers were conscripted and sent to die overseas,"

Alessandria met his eyes.

"One night, my mother tucked me into bed, gave me a goodnight kiss. Then the soldiers from the Noble House came. They broke back the door, went to grab me. My mother... jumped in front. She was cut in two. I flee. I watched my village burn in the distance,"

"I'm sorry,"

"So am I. We died by the hands of the people who were meant to protect us,"

"What House may I ask?"

119

"I don't know. I flee to other Noble Houses and begged them to save me,"

"They kicked me to the curb. One even broke my leg,"

"What about the Inquisition?"

"I was lying there dying in the streets and a woman picked me up and took me to the Order,"

"Was that a good thing?"

"They beat us daily, whipped us and burned us. I was five years old. So, Lady Fireheart I will never apologize for my hate towards the Nobility,"

Without thinking, Alessandria kissed Nemesio.

"You don't have to apologise,"

The Inquisitor didn't move away.

"What do we do now?"

"Oh, Nemesio. I don't know. The Queen…"

"Is here," a woman said from the other side of the Lighthouse.

Alessandria stood up and smiled as she stood up to see her friend. In her night black robe and two thick heavy golden swords on her back.

Stepping over to the Queen, Alessandria hugged her. Breathing in her sweet flowery perfume and feeling the smooth expensive leather of the cloak. Staring at the queen's face, Alessandria had to be jealous of her stunning looks.

Nemesio knelt before her.

"Rise Inquisitor," she commanded with supremacy. Alessandria marvelled at how the Queen managed to say every single word with such power and authority.

"Thank you for coming. What took you?"

"Alessandria," the Queen passed her a letter.

The Dominicus Procurator read it quickly, "I Mage of the Blessed Earth, Holy Water, Divine Air and Scared Metal, bah, bah, bah…"

Alessandria stared at the Queen.

"What is it?"

"Inquisitor, I have managed to get the Mages of all the other Orders to agree to join us in destroying the Order of the Sacred Fire. I have outlawed them and their operatives. And the House of the Earthers is no more. They have been stripped of all honour and titles,"

Alessandria grabbed the Queen by the elbow and took her over to the edge of the Lighthouse. Breathing in the salty sea air and looking over the harbour.

"Thank you for doing this. I'm sorry at the costs it must have caused,"

"You know, don't you?"

"I've heard rumours. How secure is your reign?"

"I have been on the throne for 10 months. But I went too quick. Legalising abortion, equal rights for woman, all the gay laws and ending the war against Mortisical. It was too much, too soon,"

"What? You saved thousands of lives. You allowed your citizens to be treated right and equally.

You allowed common women to be treated like people, not objects,"

"My power is nothing. In the courts, my word is meaningless. The Houses, the Orders and the Church hold all the power. Even in my own castle, traitors are waiting to kill me. This hasn't helped me,"

"It didn't mean I am any less grateful. But why do this?"

"Daniel helped me a long time ago. I have to repay the favour,"

Nemesio walked over.

"Are we going to do something?"

Alessandria turned to him.

"Yes, I'm going to rescue Daniel and rip the heart out of that mage,"

CHAPTER 20

Listening to the screaming battle in the distance with the shouting of orders, screams of the dying and clanging of swords and explosions of the gunpowder. Alessandria smiled as she realized this was happening. The chamber militants of the Inquisitorial Orders, the Queen's army and even her own House forces had united to free her brother.

Whilst she was under no delusions the Orders couldn't care less about Daniel, it still meant something that they came.

Returning her focus to the forest around her, Alessandria looked around at the thick dark knobby trees that littered the forest. Their fresh flowers and pine trees making the air fresh and earthy.

Along with the warm damp morning wind whipping through the forests. Making the tree branches crash into each other.

However, with Nemesio kneeling at her side, Alessandria knew she had more important things to focus on. A few metres from her was the immense solid stone Temple of the Order of the Sacred Fire. It was more of a Fortress than anything else.

Nemesio had managed to thankfully guide her through the forest to avoid the depleted patrols. Yet even with the Inquisition focusing on the front gate where the army was attacking. It still left a lot of people to guard Daniel.

The Inquisition had rumoured there was a secret passage only the mage knew about and she told him about it years ago after a few drinks. Now, he only needed to remember it.

Alessandria hated the whole concept of secret passages. She didn't deny their usefulness but they were often kept as such bad secrets. Your enemy already had them guarded before you got to them.

Although, what played on her mind was Daniel's health. She knew the Inquisition often left its prisoners broken and insane. She wasn't going to let that happen to him. Not so soon after they had grown closer. And she needed him to be Lord Fireheart.

"I remember," Nemesio announced.

Alessandria looked at him.

"Lead the way but know if my brother dies. You will join him,"

Nemesio nodded as he and Alessandria crouched through the forest over to the immense solid stone wall on the temple.

The Inquisitor started tapping on the stone and after a few moments, some of the stone melted away.

Alessandria snapped out her two large black swords.

"Are you ready, Inquisitor?"

Nemesio got out his swords and walked into the temple.

Walking along the corridors, Alessandria didn't stop to look at the temple, not even the cold yellow stone and the candles that burnt on the walls. She was here for Daniel and no one else.

As she walked, she heard her feet tap on the stone and the stone press into her boots.

"Where are the prisoners kept?"

"Around the corner," Nemesio explained.

"Heretics!" a man shouted.

Alessandria spun around.

Multiple knights in thick golden armour with massive red shields charged at them.

"Go! We cannot fight them!"

Nemesio led the way.

Alessandria ran down the corridor.

The immense mass of metal chasing her clanged and banged.

Alessandria chopped down the candles as she ran.

She heard a knight fall in the darkness.

A few more seconds at best.

They turned a corner.

To see tens of wooden doors.

Nemesio kept running.

It made sense to keep Daniel in a better prison block.

Alessandria kept running.

She looked at the odd prison cell as she ran.

She knew some of these people.

The sounds of Knights got louder. There were more of them now.

Alessandria stopped and started to open some of the doors.

The prisoners walked out naked and fragile into the corridor.

"In the Name of the Blueheart!" Alessandria screamed as she started running again.

The prisoners broke out into a frenzy.

Alessandria heard the prisoners breaking doors and stone to make weapons. Anything to serve their House once more.

She looked at Nemesio.

He was still running.

More knights thundered towards them.

Nemesio turned another corner.

Alessandria followed.

She was tackled by a male Inquisitor in fiery armour.

He punched her rapidly.

He kicked her.

His hands wrapped around her throat.

Alessandria forced her swords through his armour.

His blood covering her face.

She jumped up and started running again.

Stone exploded around her as gunshots were fired.

Nemesio stopped outside a massive cast iron door.

Alessandria turned around and threw her sword at the two shooters.

It went straight through them like a skewer.

Alessandria ran to Nemesio.

"You ready?" he asked.

She nodded.

The Inquisitor broke the lock.

They stormed into the chamber.

She looked around.

The massive stone chamber was empty.

She focused.

She saw Daniel, bloodied and tied to a cross in the middle.

Three Inquisitors stabbed him.

Alessandria screamed.

She charged at them.

An almighty blow of her sword shattered the body of one man.

Nemesio ripped the head of another Inquisitor.

The last one punched Alessandria to the ground.

He kicked her again and again.

He grabbed his spear.

Alessandria grabbed it, jumped up and forced the spear through him.

The chamber was empty.

The Dominicus Procurator rushed over to Daniel. She brushed his bloodied, cutted face with her hands.

His eyes opened weakly.

Alessandria kissed him and looked at his battered, broken body full of cuts and stab wounds. Quickly she looked at his arms, it was impossible to tell what was old and what was new.

Nemesio cut Daniel free.

Daniel fell into Alessandria's arms as she lowered him to the ground and held him in her arms.

Daniel simply stared at her. She didn't know what he was thinking but she didn't care. He was safe.

When Alessandria looked up, she saw an elderly lady with fine golden robes holding some sort of flaming bottle.

"Mage!" Nemesio screamed.

"Traitor! Heretic! We must die. When I drop this, we will all burn!"

She raised the bottle.

She threw it.

Her head cracked as a wooden staff stabbed her.

Hellen stormed in.

She whacked the flaming bottle away.

It cracked.

Burning alcohol flooded onto the far wall of the chamber.

Hellen thumbed the Mage's head a final time.

"That felt good!" Hellen proclaimed.

Alessandria returned her attention to Daniel.

He was staring at Nemesio's armour.

He started to scream and scream.

He started to scratch himself.

More blood poured out.

"Hellen!" Alessandria screamed.

She rushed over and forced the thick glowing yellow potion down his throat.

Within seconds, Daniel stopped but she knew he didn't want to.

Her brother stared at her and weakly stroked her face.

Alessandria took out Daniel's dulled blade and place it in his pocket.

He smiled.

"You came for me,"

"I wouldn't abandon you brother. I need you to be Lord Fireheart first,"

Daniel laughed up some blood.

"You shouldn't be here,"

"Why not Daniel?"

"Alexis, this was planned. You attack the Order. The Earthers attack our castle,"

"There's no one defending it?"

"No, Nemesio. All our forces are here,"

Alessandria helped Daniel up.

"Can you fight brother?"

"I can try,"

CHAPTER 21

I gripped Alessandria tight as her horse stormed towards our castle. My vision was a crazy blur of thick brown trees and the odd flash of fire.

Burying my face into Alessandria's back, I pressed my nose into her cold black leather cloak. The leather chilled my skin but I needed the cold.

I fought hard to suppress the memories of my torture. The whipping, stabbing and other unspeakable horrors. The dogs, the dogs. The touching, touching. No, no, no.

I needed to stay calm. My family needed me. Alessandria needed me.

Biting my lip, I gave a small scream as my arms burned with pain from old and new wounds. Then I screamed as I felt the pain from the stab wounds dripping blood on my chest and stomach.

I felt the wind whip past us as we ride but I just wanted to… I quickly shook the thought away.

Shaking my head, I realised that the sanity potion must be failing. If I didn't get help soon, my mind and body would break. Again, I wanted to scream as I felt an immense pressure press against my mind.

Turning my head slightly, I saw Hellen. She smiled at me. Normally, I would smile back. I liked her. One of the few people I cared about. But I didn't care at that moment. I wanted peace.

Looking slightly past Hellen, I saw that... Inquisitor. The pressure built more. My heart pounded.

I wanted to kill him. This was all his fault.

Forcing myself to reclaim focused, I grabbed my dulled blade from my pocket and made myself play with it.

Alessandria gave me a gentle jab in the ribs. Clearly forgetting my stab wounds. Looking up, my vision cleared to see our castle ablaze. The mighty towers turned to ash. Thick black smoke veiling the morning sky and our lungs.

Alessandria stepped off the horse. Making me fall off. My face splashed onto the ground. I needed to kill something!

My sister came to help me. I kicked her away. I wasn't sorry.

Forcing myself up, my eyes widened as I saw the hundreds of Earther soldiers in their silver Knight armour. They all turned towards us.

My dulled blade spun quicker.

Alessandria stepped protectively in front of us. Drawing out her sword.

One larger knight in thick golden armour stepped towards us. The rest of his forces pointed their spears and swords towards us.

"You should not have come here Earthers. This is the sanctuary of the Firehearts, and it shall not fall," Alessandria calmly stated.

The large knight took off his helmet and I wanted to slaughter him as he revealed himself to be Geoff.

This was pathetic. He was his father's puppet and now he would die for it. That was my promise.

My dulled blade span as fast as it could.

"Fireheart, you are wrong. You have bought this upon yourself,"

"We have not. The Earthers have made their decisions. You created your problems. This was punishment. We could have been united in marriage. You betrayed us so we took revenge,"

"Now you will pay. You and the freak shall die. The freak I will torture first,"

Geoff's forces took a step closer.

"You are four against hundreds. You will die, and for what? Your mother will be dead soon enough,"

Geoff raised his hand and waved.

A grand explosion destroyed half the castle.

The castle burned.

Clumps of stone fell onto the ground.

The air stunk of cooked meat and gunpowder.

Alessandria smiled.

"Your poor father. He was in there. You tried to kill him. You backstabber,"

"I did not try. I did kill him,"

"Your father is clever. He would want to kidnap my mother, not kill her. Not until she has signed over the land and our military contracts. Unlike you, your father is clever,"

Geoff looked to the ground.

"These men are loyal to me. I will kill him and your Mother,"

"Kill them," Geoff ordered.

"Wait!" Nemesio commanded.

Even a reminder of him being around caused my mind to crack even more.

"Alessandria Fireheart, why did your brother get kicked out of the military?"

Even I had no idea how that thing of an Inquisitor even had a suspicion about my exile.

She looked at me.

I nodded.

It might be the only chance we have at surviving this.

Alessandria looked at Geoff and the knights. She walked back behind me.

"You see Geoff, my brother is a Flesheater. There are two types, one can see flesh memories. The other has... more interesting abilities. Then sometimes you get extremely rare mutations that give you a person who can do both,"

"So?"

"So, Daniel was on a mission in Mortisical with twenty other men. They were ambushed by over a hundred foes. They almost all died. That's when Daniel's other abilities manifested. He killed everyone even his own men,"

Geoff took a step back.

"Kill them now!"

The Knight stormed towards us.

Alessandria turned to me.

"Daniel, break the bottle. Lose control. I beg you,"

I didn't want to.
But the knights raised their spears and swords.
I broke the bottle.
The mind shattered.
All my dark thoughts flooded my mind.
My bones hardened.
I felt my eyes burning red.
Magical energy crackled around me.
I felt my teeth turn into fangs.
I only wanted to kill.
My hands burned and twisted into talons.
Flying forward, I jumped onto a knight.
Forcing my teeth through its armour.
Feasting on his flesh.
I jumped onto another knight.
Slashing my way through the armour.
Other knights screamed.
Other knights stabbed me.
It didn't matter.
I charged into the army of knights.
Ripping into their flesh.
Their blood painting my body.
My body warm with their flesh.
Their bones crushed and snapped.
My talons dripping with muscle and blood.
My vision turned red with blood.
I turned to look at Geoff.
My mouth was full of the flesh of his friends.
I charged at him.
He swung his sword.
I caught it and snapped it.
Smiling at him, I thrusted a talon through him.

He stared into my bestial eyes.

Ripping off his head, I munched on his once beautiful face.

Before I devoured the body. His bones cracking in my mouth.

Alessandria ran over to me.

"Kill them all. Hellen will stay with you. Protect her. I and Nemesio will save Mother,"

Forcing some sanity to return to me, I nodded before I whacked some Knights. Cracking their armour to get to the sweet flesh inside.

CHAPTER 22

Climbing over the shatter smouldering grey blocks of stone, Alessandria and Nemesio climbed into the decimated remains of the ballroom.

Alessandria looked with wide eyes as the ballroom had come crashing down with the walls being torn open. Making the once stunning domed roof collapse. Only the area near her Mother's throne had survived.

Yet the explosion and the smouldering ruins caused thick columns of smoke to rise up and veil the sky and room.

The sun tried to shine through the thick veil of smoke to no avail. It was far too thick. Leaving the castle in a dim light.

Alessandria climbed to the bottom of the pile of rubble. Being surprised by the height of the rubble. Nemesio joined her but Alessandria started to walk in the direction of the golden throne. She needed to find her mother.

As she walked, the thick smoke coated her lungs and skin and she heard the screaming and tearing of metal in the distance.

Whilst she knew getting Daniel to break the bottle on his Flesheater ability was the right decision. It didn't mean she felt good about it. Her brother had been tortured by an extreme organisation for hours upon hours. He was fragile. And she felt as if she had pushed him off an edge.

Whatever happened next Alessandria knew she was around this time and she wasn't going to let Daniel be alone. But first Lord Earther needed to die.

Turning her attention back to the shattered ballroom, the smoke started to clear. Revealing the shape of a woman on the floor resting her head on the throne.

Alessandria rushed forward. To see her Mother lying on her golden throne in her blood soaked robes surrounded by broken wine bottles.

Alessandria went to hug her Mother but Kinaaz held her wine bottle like a club. Pointing it towards the smoke.

The Dominicus Procurator didn't need words to understand her Mother. The Lord Earther was waiting for them in the smoke.

Nemesio came over to join her.

Slowly, a large man walked out of the smoke armoured in thick black Knight armour with a sword and shield as tall as Alessandria.

"Fair Alessandria, my son is dead?" the Lord Haben Earther uttered through his helmet.

She nodded.

"Thank you,"

"Why? Why do any of this?"

"Lady Alessandria, there is a war coming. Ordericous will be besieged. We must be ready. We must kill all our weaker elements if we are to survive,"

"My House is not weak,"

"Perhaps not. But you and the Queen will not do what's right for the Kingdom,"

"And you will?"

"Of course, every man, women and child will be conscripted in service. We will conquer Mortisical before they can conquer us,"

Kinaaz threw a wine bottle at him.

"Listen here Lord, you are deluded. My husband fought in those wars. War will get us nowhere,"

"Coming from the Lady Fireheart who makes all her money from war contracts,"

Alessandria had had enough. She stormed forwards.

Nemesio did too.

She swung her blade.

Haben slammed down his shield.

Magic crackled around it.

Throwing Alessandria back.

She slammed into the cold floor. Small shards of rock cut her face.

Nemesio swung his blade.

Haben whacked him with the shield.

He walked towards Alessandria.

Kinaaz threw some wine bottles.

Haben slammed his shield onto the ground.

More magic crackled.

All Kinaaz's remaining bottles exploded.

The air was filled with shattered shards of glass and the smell of fruity wine.

Kinaaz jumped up.

Alessandria and Nemesio joined her.

They all charged at Haben.

He raised his sword. Swinging it at Alessandria.

She ducked.

She grabbed Haben's sword hand.

He tried to wave her free.

Nemesio slacked with his sword.

It didn't dent the Lord.

Haben threw Alessandria across the ballroom.

He slammed his shield down.

Sending Nemesio flying.

Alessandria landed with a thud. Her head hitting the ground.

She felt the blood dripping down the back of her head.

The Dominicus Procurator looked for her Mother.

Kinaaz was gone.

Haben looked around.

Out from nowhere Kinaaz jumped on Haben.

He screamed.

Alessandria didn't understand why.

She stood and ran over to Haben.

She slowed down when she got closer. As she saw smoke rising from Haben's armour. Beautiful golden magical light shone from Kinaaz's hands.

Haben continued to scream as Kinaaz started to turn his armour and flesh into gold.

Nemesio stumbled over to Alessandria. Placing a warm hand on her shoulder.

"Your Mother's an Alchemist?"

"How do you think she can afford her drinking?"

Alessandria really didn't want to get into all the times she had had to cash in gold to get wine money for her mother.

Haben gave a final almighty scream as his entire body was turned to gold.

"Inquisitor, your gun," Kinaaz ordered.

He threw it to her.

Kinaaz aimed it at the Haben Statue's head and fired.

The golden form of Haben shattered into tens of large shards.

Kinaaz picked up a piece of his shield and: "This should get me a few crates of wine,"

Alessandria wandered over to the shards and kicked them.

"I'll cash them in after Justin's funeral. I'll give half the money to the children's charities and the Veterans charities,"

Her Mother nodded.

Alessandria knew her mother didn't care where the money went but Alessandria was definitely going to keep some of the other half. Money is a precious resource when it comes to changing laws.

More rocks fell as Alessandria turn to see Hellen running towards her.

Alessandria almost gagged as Hellen smelt of blood and corpses.

"We have a problem! We have a problem!"

"What Hellen? Calm down!"

Hellen took a few deep breaths.

"It's Daniel. I barely managed to knock him out,"

"Why?"

"He's gone mad. His mind is broken. He's screaming,"

"Get him to the Queen's Palace!"

As all four of them run off, Alessandria realised she had failed. Her brother had fallen. She didn't protect him. But maybe there was still time to heal him.

CHAPTER 23

Taking off her cloak, Alessandria shook off the thick layer of rain that covered the leather cloak. The water formed little puddles on the polished white marble of the Queen's Medical Wing.

Passing her cloak to a little male servant, he gracefully walked away. Raising her look Alessandria looked around for a nurse, doctor or even another servant. She needed to find Daniel. But she only saw sterile white polished marble walls and pillars.

Although Alessandria did get a kick out of seeing a picture of her father on the wall for his so-called contributions to medicine. She had no idea what her father did except give a few thousand coins to open the first children's hospital in Ordericous.

Stepping forward, Alessandria almost slipped on the puddles of water and she started to elegantly walk through the medical wing. Passing white marble wall after wall.

As she walked the rain outside lashed against the stained glass roof. Depicting various saints and founders of modern medicine. They were beautiful even if Alessandria despised faith.

A scream came from down the corridor.

She started to walk towards it. Thinking about the secure wards she had walked on cases for her House. The people on those wards were… disturbed.

More screaming echoed down the chamber.

Alessandria hated the sound. Tears wanted to flood down her face but she wasn't going to let them. Not until she knew what was going on.

Loud bangs and more screams echoed around her.

The air smelt of disgusting chemicals used to hide the notes of urine, fear and death. She wasn't going to let Daniel die here.

Her footsteps got louder as she stormed down the corridor until a tall man in some awful bright white cloth or suit stepped out. Alessandria gagged as he smelt of rotten flesh and toxic chemicals.

Despite her better judgement, Alessandria stopped in front of the chief medic.

"Lady Alessandria for Daniel?"

Alessandria rolled her eyes at his overly formal, boring voice.

"Yes, Chief Officer,"

"Excellent, the patient…"

"Daniel,"

"Of course, Daniel is for lack of better term broken,"

Alessandria wanted to know what sort of doctor he was. What comfort did he bring the dying?

"My Lady, I apologise if I have offended. I usually have my lessers deal with people,"

Alessandria heard the typical wood tapping against the marble as Hellen walked in.

"Perfect timing. Dearest Chief Officer, look at the woman behind me. Tell me about my brother or I get her to thump you with her stick,"

"Of course, Daniel is experiencing an extreme case of Post-Traumatic Stress,"

"I've seen that in my war friends but never like this,"

"His autism plus the extreme stimulation from the Flesheater… ability played with his mind. Add to that the stress and irritation the social world and his family being in danger. You can imagine the resulting effect from this experience,"

"Started treatment yet doc?" Hellen asked.

"They let commoners in here?"

"Common to the bone, oh me. Common and proud,"

Alessandria smiled.

"I'll even spit on the floor for ya if you want,"

Alessandria waved her friend quiet.

"Have you started treatment?" Alessandria asked.

"There is no treatment,"

"Yes, there is. I checked up on many of my friends in PTS centres,"

"My apologies Lady Fireheart, Daniel cannot be treated. He thinks everyone is a danger to him and… we have had to restrain him and remove his fingernails. We cut them very short, but they were still effective cutting tools,"

Hellen rubbed Alessandria's back.

Immense screams filled the corridor again.

"What could heal my brother?"

"There have been many theories proposed about extreme PTS,"

"Do not test me here, Officer. Give me possible solutions or my friend here will whack you with her big stick,"

"I could whack her with mine,"

Alessandria punched the man.

"My brother is screaming in there. This is no time to make jokes,"

"Fine, fine, fine. What makes him relax?"

Alessandria looked at Hellen.

She shrugged.

A tear swelled up in her eye as Alessandria realised and understood for a brief moment how tough Daniel's life was. Always on edge, always concerned about how he would react to something, a noise, a person. Always concerned about being attacked by Justin or one of his many bullies. No wonder he had never relaxed, he was always on guard and so tense.

Now, Alessandria understood. She even understood why Daniel was tense in her presence. She never protected him; she was never there for him. If one sibling could beat him up. Then as far as he was concerned there was no reason, she couldn't attack him.

"There is no one, Officers. My brother doesn't relax around anyone,"

Hellen tapped Alessandria's leg with her stick.

"Ya know, what about Harrison? He's in the castle, right?"

Delight filled Alessandria.

She hugged Hellen.

They started to walk away, before Alessandria firmly said to the Chief Medical Officer, "Keep my brother alive or your death will be a painful few weeks!"

CHAPTER 24

As Alessandria looked around her eyes narrowed. Looking at each of the red, black and gold horse-drawn carriages. With strong muscular shirtless men banging hammers and other tools on them. Trying to fix and maintain these mighty carriages for the Queen.

Her and Hellen kept walking further into the engineering hall with the well spotted black greasy wall and the chipped dirty stone floor.

Alessandria turned her head to see Hellen staring or inspecting the men. Whilst she could not blame her friend in the slightest, she had heard enough stories to want to stay well away from these men.

Continuing to walk between the twenty carriages being stored and repaired here, Alessandria frowned as she heard all the hissing, banging and shouting of the men. She laughed to herself as she imagined Daniel being down here. He would hate it. He would have a stress attack or something. Where was Harrison?

Despite, Hellen's drive something being an irritant. Alessandria had to praise her ability to seduce men when the Queen's Guards refused to confirm if Harrison was here.

As her leather boots walked on oil and soot, Alessandria's heart beat a little faster. The last time she had seen Harrison was a week or two before the lies. Even then she had made out with him and told him to leave her alone afterwards. Not her best moment but she couldn't date him not with Daniel loving him. And that's why she probably did it in the first place. To get back at the little brother who had so much of their father's time. Then it hit her.

Alessandria wanted to fall on the top as she realised where she was when Justin was beating up her mother and Daniel. And when Daniel was trying to end himself. She was too busy being a Procurator and taking advantage of her Nobility. Alessandria stopped as she realised her little princess phase had cost so much.

"Ya okay, Alexis? Ya seem a little pale,"

"Um, yes. I'll be fine,"

Alessandria saw Harrison working shirtless on the door of a massive carriage.

They walked over to him.

"Harrison Gearing," Alessandria greeted him formally.

"Wow, I know why Daniel likes him," Hellen said as she looked at his tight, sooted well-muscled chest.

"Alessandria Fireheart," Harrison said as he threw an oily rag on the floor. "Why are you here? Coming to honour the family tradition and threaten me,"

"Harrison, I am not my brother. I wouldn't hurt you,"

"Oh you Nobles. Always lying. You did me just to get back at your brother and then you hurt me. Even worse, I find out my best friend tried to kill himself and you did nothing!"

Other engineers looked at her as Harrison shouted.

"I know I've made some stupid mistakes. And believe me I hate myself for it. I hate myself so much right now. But let me make it right,"

"It's too late. Get out of my Halls. I have work to do," Harrison said as he picked up his metal took box, his muscles flexing, and he walked away.

"Daniel needs you," Alessandria said. "He tried to save us all and he's... damaged, broken. I don't know. But you were the only person he has ever loved, cared for and relaxed around. Please help him,"

"Hellen, is she lying?"

"Na, it's bad, Harry,"

"You two know each other?"

"Of course when I was straight, she was great,"

"Will you help Daniel please?"

"I will come with you but know this Alessandria Fireheart. I am doing this for Daniel, not you. And you will confess what you did to him,"

"Of course,"

"I mean it,"

Alessandria nodded fiercely.

"On my honour as a Dominicus Procurator,"

"Take me to him and be ready to confess your sins,"

CONNOR WHITELEY

CHAPTER 25

Walking through the castle, Alessandria guided Harrison through the immense medical Wing. She still wasn't pleased with the glaring sterile white marble with the gold veins running through some of them.

And as for the stained glass roof the afternoon sun was beaming through it. Making Alessandria look like some sort of rainbow unicorn.

Then she shook her head and took a few deep breaths, breathing in the chemicals and polish fumes of the corridor they walked through. Maybe she was just annoyed at herself for her little princess phase.

She mocked herself for those few months were did what every other Noble child did, abuse their power, sleep with everyone and think themselves better than everyone else.

Alessandria's face turned pale as she remembered how furious her father had been. At the time, she didn't care, not when he was so busy with his Lord duties and Daniel. But now she knew he was making sure Daniel could cope in the world.

That's probably why she became a Procurator. Redemption? Sorrow? She didn't know but she knew she hated herself for not being there for Daniel.

Looking at Harrison briefly, who was now wearing a very loose black t-shirt, she started to wonder why Justin had been so hard on him. He didn't deserve it. But she started to wonder would he ever forgive her and her family. Only Daniel ever treated him right and fairly. Whatever happened today would hopefully start a path to healing but what a long road that would be.

Returning her attention to the corridor, Daniel's screams filled the chamber and Alessandria, Hellen and Harrison passed a tall thin nurse in blood soaked robes as another nurse struggled to stop the blood pouring out from her severed fingers.

Alessandria gave a small smile at the thought of Daniel biting off the nurse's fingers. She wanted to praise him but this wasn't the time. Nor the thing to praise him for.

The screams got louder and louder as they walked.

Looking at Harrison, the Dominicus Procurator was amazed that whilst she had slowed at hearing the screams. Harrison had stayed strong and kept walking.

A loud bang followed by another and another and another sounded from Daniel's door.

As the three of them got closer, Alessandria's stomach grew tight and her skin went cold. A foul taste of chemicals entered her mouth. Sweat poured off her forehead.

When they reached the thick wooden door with three large padlocks, Alessandria looked around for the Chief Officer. She didn't like him but she needed him. He wasn't anywhere to be seen.

Alessandria nodded to Hellen.

Smiling Hellen grabbed her big stick, stuck it in each padlock and popped each of them like they were made from glass.

Alessandria placed a caring and sorry hand on Harrison's shoulder and said: "Thank you for doing this,"

With that Hellen opened the door, Harrison walked it.

Looking from the doorway, she saw Daniel screaming in the corner, bashing himself and cursing his torturer. His skin was bleeding and wrecked. His eyes were black and bloodshot.

Harrison walked over to the large soft silk bed and sat on there. His back rested on the pillowed headboard.

Daniel saw him.

His head shaking, unsure of what he saw.

He crawled over to the bed, leaving a trail of blood on the floor, snuggled into Harrison and fell asleep.

CHAPTER 26

As Justin's body finished turning to the ashes and the flames went out in the immense domed church with golden Holy light illuminating everything, people started to leave.

Alessandria stared at the altar watching the last of her brother's bones fall apart. Breathing in the last of the smell of cooking flesh and burned leather. And the feeling of the coating of ash over her skin.

The sister part of her didn't like this. Burning Justin and throwing him in the river so there wouldn't be any trace of him.

But as a sister and daughter, she understood it. Justin was a stain on her family, a monster who needed to be killed. Now, her only hope was looking forward to the future and the healing of her family.

Alessandria looked around the domed church. Seeing the smooth stone walls with nothing on them. She rolled her eyes at the boring nature of the church. Even as she stretched her neck and looked up. The domed ceiling was nothing but some so-called holy white marble. She didn't like religion but she at least wanted to see a stained glass window.

This really was the beginning of a new chapter in her's and her family's life. She needed everyone and she loved them all. Yet these past few days reminded her of why she needed to change the law. It was in the interest of the House, her people and the country to get Daniel Lorded.

Alessandria smiled as she thought about the dangers of what she wanted to do. She would have to take on everyone from the Nobility to the Inquisition to the Church to get the law passed. But it didn't matter nothing happened more than her family.

Turning around Alessandria saw all her family there her mother with an empty bottle of wine, Hellen with her oversized stick and even the Inquisitor was there to pay his respects.

In all honesty, Alessandria had no idea what she felt about Nemesio. She kissed him but that didn't excuse his past behaviour. But he was trying so that had to count for something.

Then she looked at Daniel, her beautiful brother, he looked at her in his black leather cloak and she wondered how it was only a week ago he was screaming and suffering.

However, Harrison calmed him enough and he was responding to therapies. Alessandria knew there was a long way to go but she would be there for her brother this time.

She walked over to Daniel who was clinging to Harrison's arm and she admitted Harrison looked great in his black suit.

"Daniel, it is good to see you up and well. Thank you Harrison for everything,"

Harrison nodded to her.

"And Daniel I have to confess something. This isn't easy to admit but I remember why I wasn't there for you growing up. I was jealous so I went out of my way to get revenge for you taking up father's time. Which I now know was important. So, I am sorry. And I'm sorry for sleeping with Harrison… and doing… more than sleeping,"

Daniel gave a cheeky grin and said: "Oh Alessandria. Harrison told me the night of the party. We laughed and laughed about it," Daniel took a step closer to Alessandria. "Now, stop hating yourself. You have to remember us autistic people don't care about the pointless things you do,"

Alessandria just stared at Daniel in equal shock and amazement.

"Now, I must leave. I have military contracts to sign. I must get back to my routine," Daniel started to walk away using Harrison as a wall between him and Nemesio.

"He seems better and happy," Hellen said as she watched them walk away and lent on Alessandria's shoulder.

"Yes, I haven't seen him happy in a long, long time,"

"Do ya think they're a couple now?"

"I don't know… but I will support him whatever he does,"

"Was Harrison ever good in the…" Hellen started as Alessandria placed her hand over Hellen's mouth.

"My beautiful best friend, loyal to a fault and so inappropriate,"

"What more could a gal want in a friend?"

"Nothing. You're perfect as you are my friend. Stay safe," Alessandria said as she hugged Hellen goodbye.

Alessandria walked towards the stone archway outside when she smelt strong fruity wine from behind her. It was no surprise to see her mother standing there.

Her mother looked to the floor.

"My... beautiful daughter. Just thank you. You saved me, this House. And I am going to get help,"

Alessandria hugged her mother.

"You get the help you need and I'll get it out the press,"

"Thank you, I'm going to stop drinking. I'm safe now, and so's Daniel,"

"We're all safe now. I will protect this family and I will be there for both of you,"

"We're here for you too. And I need to go to a meeting now,"

Kinaaz started to walk away when Alessandria said: "I'm proud of you mum,"

"I'm proud of you too,"

As soon as Kinaaz had left the church, Alessandria continued to walk towards the door before an overly posh voice asked: "Lady Fireheart?"

All Alessandria wanted was to go back to her quarter's at the Palace and sleep.

Turning around, she saw a tall man dressed in bright metallic blue robes with a strange fist symbol on the front that she didn't recognise. And the man stunk of rich earthy perfumes and oils.

"I am Lady Alessandria Fireheart, Dominicus Procurator of the House of Fireheart, who addresses me?"

"I am a representative of the new House of the Illuminated Fists,"

She knew that name.

"Annalise's Family?"

"Yes, my Lady. After the thankful destruction of the Earthers, the glorious Queen promoted the Blood Family to Noble status,"

Alessandria smiled. On the few occasions, she had met Annalise's family, they always seemed good, honest people. That could only serve her in her ends.

"That is splendid news but I must question why are you meeting me and not my mother,"

"Because my Lady, the Lord and Lady Blood have heard of your ambitions to change the laws and they pledge their support with you. When the matter is raised in the court,"

"Then they have my most gracious thoughts. Give them my regards and take… this as a gift," Alessandria picked up one of the bottles of wine on the floor. The servant took it, bowed and left.

Despite her delight that she had an ally in the courts, Alessandria just wanted to go. She started to walk to towards the archway to the outside.

"You're popular," a slim woman said in an expensive purple silk cloak. The woman's sweet perfume made Alessandria smiled.

"You are quite adept at stealth, my Queen,"

"I try. Has your House made plans yet? You have no castle, no home. I have already reclaimed the land and the people,"

"My mother knew you would have a plan,"

"Your mother is clever. That is why I have made a new set of decrees this morning to my Court's anger,"

"Can you afford to make more enemies?"

"That is my problem, my dear. Your Mother is effectively Governor of your Land now. Your brother has control over your military contracting business and all of you now live in the castle. Working for me directly,"

"And me?"

The Queen waved over Nemesio.

"My Queen," he bowed.

"Inquisitor, I am sorry to hear about your Order. Rest assured, the rest of your former Order has been killed or the ones loyal to the throne have been taken into the Queen's Procurator,"

"Thank you, your Majesty. How many?"

"Three were taken in,"

Nemesio gave a quiet nod.

"And me?" Alessandria repeated.

The Queen looked her dead in the eye.

"You have always been good to me and I thank you for that. As you know my reign hangs by a thread. I have more enemies than friends inside and out of the castle. I do not know who to trust,"

The Queen handed Alessandria and Nemesio two black metal circles with her head on both sides. Alessandria shivered at the touch of the metal.

"These are my seals. With these, anyone questioning you will be dealt with as if they are questioning me,"

"Why give us these?" Nemesio inquired.

"There is a conspiracy to kill me. They seek to reverse my liberal laws and go even further. If they succeed, there will be no equality, freedom of speech and the common folk will be slaves to their new ruler. I love my subjects; I cannot allow that to happen. Will you help me?"

"Of course," they both returned.

AUTHOR'S NOTE

Thank you for reading. I really hope you enjoyed it.

Personally, I loved writing this book because I've been playing around with the idea for this book for a few months now.

I felt drawn to the story or series because you had the nobility, a gay autistic character and a sister who knew nothing about her family.

Originally, I got the idea for the book from Lindsay Buroker's Agent of the Crown Series. Which is a great fantasy series about an Inquisitor meeting a Nobleman's son. Then I started to think about how I could adapt it. Leaving me with the reverse and I introduced an abusive son, a gay and autistic character and I made it my own.

Also, I've always loved the idea of nobility, not the disgusting ways they treated people, but the riches and political intrigue have always been a source of ideas.

In the beginning, Justin wasn't meant to be a bad character but when I started to write it. It just popped out and I'm so glad I did it.

It definitely added to the pain of the characters and if I was Alessandria I would have felt the same. I would have been shocked but hated myself for not knowing about Justin's darker side.

Also, Nemesio in the beginning, I always knew he was going to be difficult at first, but I never intended for him to be so… annoying. But I think it made him an interesting character. Not someone I would like to meet until towards the end. But interesting, nevertheless.

However, I think my favourite character to write about was Daniel because he is different, and he has been through so much. Yet it was good to write about the different ways he sees and experiences the world.

Although, I am looking forward to writing the rest of the series. I'm especially interested in finding out what happens between Daniel and Harrison.

I also found it interesting because I never usually write gay characters or neurodivergent characters. Sorry about the term, I study psychology at University as I write this series.

Anyway, I really hope you've enjoyed the book and hopefully I'll see you in the next one!

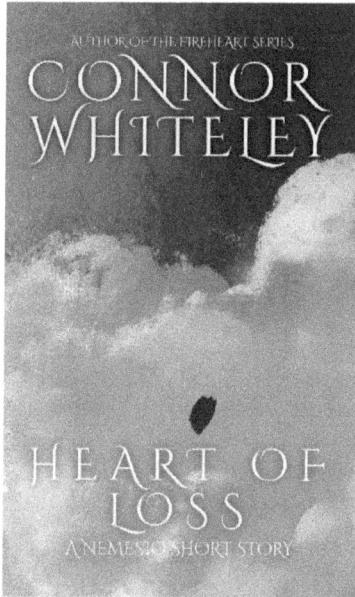

GET YOUR FREE AND EXCLUSIVE
SHORT STORY NOW! LEARN ABOUT
NEMESIO'S PAST!

https://www.subscribepage.com/fireheart

Thank you for reading.

I hoped you enjoyed it.

If you want a FREE book and keep up to date about new books and project. Then please sign up for my newsletter at https://www.subscribepage.com/fireheart

Have a great day.

About the author:

Connor Whiteley is the author of over 30 books in the sci-fi fantasy, nonfiction psychology and books for writer's genre and he is a Human Branding Speaker and Consultant.

He is a passionate warhammer 40,000 reader, psychology student and author.

Who narrates his own audiobooks and he hosts The Psychology World Podcast.

All whilst studying Psychology at the University of Kent, England.

Also, he was a former Explorer Scout where he gave a speech to the Maltese President in August 2018 and he attended Prince Charles' 70th Birthday Party at Buckingham Palace in May 2018.

Plus, he is a self-confessed coffee lover!

SHORT STORIES BY CONNOR WHITELEY

Blade of The Emperor

Arbiter's Truth

The Bloodied Rose

Asmodia's Wrath

Other books by Connor Whiteley:

The Fireheart Fantasy Series

Heart of Fire

Heart of Lies

More Coming Soon!

The Garro Series- Fantasy/Sci-fi

GARRO: GALAXY'S END

GARRO: RISE OF THE ORDER

GARRO: END TIMES

GARRO: SHORT STORIES

GARRO: COLLECTION

GARRO: HERESY

GARRO: FAITHLESS

GARRO: DESTROYER OF WORLDS

GARRO: COLLECTIONS BOOK 4-6

GARRO: MISTRESS OF BLOOD

GARRO: BEACON OF HOPE

GARRO: END OF DAYS

Winter Series- Fantasy Trilogy Books

WINTER'S COMING

WINTER'S HUNT

WINTER'S REVENGE

WINTER'S DISSENSION

Miscellaneous:

THE ANGEL OF RETURN

THE ANGEL OF FREEDOM

Companion guides:

BIOLOGICAL PSYCHOLOGY 2ND
EDITION WORKBOOK

COGNITIVE PSYCHOLOGY 2ND
EDITION WORKBOOK

SOCIOCULTURAL PSYCHOLOGY 2ND
EDITION WORKBOOK

ABNORMAL PSYCHOLOGY 2ND
EDITION WORKBOOK

PSYCHOLOGY OF HUMAN
RELATIONSHIPS 2ND EDITION
WORKBOOK

HEALTH PSYCHOLOGY WORKBOOK

FORENSIC PSYCHOLOGY WORKBOOK

Audiobooks by Connor Whiteley:

BIOLOGICAL PSYCHOLOGY

COGNITIVE PSYCHOLOGY

SOCIOCULTURAL PSYCHOLOGY

ABNORMAL PSYCHOLOGY

PSYCHOLOGY OF HUMAN
RELATIONSHIPS

HEALTH PSYCHOLOGY

DEVELOPMENTAL PSYCHOLOGY

RESEARCH IN PSYCHOLOGY

FORENSIC PSYCHOLOGY

GARRO: GALAXY'S END

GARRO: RISE OF THE ORDER

GARRO: SHORT STORIES

GARRO: END TIMES

GARRO: COLLECTION

GARRO: HERESY

Business books:

GET YOUR FREE BOOK AT:
WWW.CONNORWHITELEY.NET

Lightning Source UK Ltd.
Milton Keynes UK
UKHW022025150721
387234UK00005B/205

9 781914 081651